ALT
SAGAS

Also by Jean Huets

The Bones You Have Cast Down
The Cosmic Tarot
Encyclopedia of Tarot (co-author Stuart R. Kaplan)
With Walt Whitman, Himself

ALT SAGAS

JEAN HUETS

gertrude m books

RICHMOND, VIRGINIA

Copyright © 2024 by Jean Huets

All rights reserved. No part of this book may be reproduced in any form, including electronic, without permission in writing from the author.

gertrude m books
an imprint of

CIRCLING RIVERS

PO Box 8291

Richmond, VA 23226

www.gertrudem.com

The characters and events in this book are fictional.

ISBN: 978-1-939530-32-5 (paper)
ISBN: 978-1-939530-33-2 (hardcover)

Library of Congress Control Number: 2023951501

Visit CirclingRivers.com and sign up to get news on other Circling Rivers / gertrude m authors and books—including events and giveaways. You'll receive a newsletter every 6-8 weeks. We never share or sell our list.

to the H-tribe:
Stella, Mike, and Jo

ALT
SAGAS

The Saga of Cuno
who was sometimes a dog and sometimes a man

SEASON OF SPRING EQUINOX

Something about our eyes, the way we used our hands, the timbre of our voices, aroused distrust among the people of this stark land. Luckily, our protector, Steini the Priest, provided us a snug cottage and traded at market for us, so we were able to keep mostly to ourselves.

Mother tended her dye pots, her wheel, and her loom, and Dad took care of our horses. We did Steini a few favors—keeping rot off his root cellar and warding off a rival priest who thought to settle not far enough away. Dad also brewed beer, which, like Mother's crafts, Steini prudently and profitably sold as products of his own household.

If Mother and Dad were content at hearth and pasture, my brother Sulgrinn and I, being young men, needed more range. We wandered the district, though it held little of interest or beauty save a few hot springs for bathing. Even where snow stubbornly held sway, seething mudpits pocked the ground, letting loose sudden burning spouts, as if an ill-wishing whale fumed under the crust of the black, jagged earth. Desolations of tree stumps, many near as wide as our cottage, told of once lofty forests felled for assembly halls which, though fit for giants, made little room for fellowship with strangers such as we were. Never did the song of wolves course the night, nor did the hoarse, vigorous calls of ravens greet us by day. Only the sharp bark of hungry foxes and the seagulls' mournful whine gave voice to the bleak land.

Sulgrinn took his fun with young farmhands, sometimes playing jokes on them, sometimes seducing them. I lay now and then with lone-dwelling spinsters or widows, or shepherdesses in remote huts. As pleasurable as that was, I looked forward most to market days. In dog form, I tussled and frolicked amongst the stalls with the children and the other dogs. The merchants tolerated my modest doggie thefts, some tossing me scraps of sausage, cheese, and other tasty tidbits. I also gathered juicy gossip, for loose talk flowed easily into my floppy ears. That's how we learned of two crafty divorces and an upcoming wedding.

It was like this. Gudrun, desiring Thord, counseled him to divorce on the grounds that his wife often wore men's britches. Gudrun herself had won a divorce on similar grounds, by sewing for her first husband a shirt cut so womanishly low, it exposed his nipples. Once free of their spouses, Thord and Gudrun announced they would marry each other.

Steini the Priest, prompted by Mother's gentle hints, got us invited to the wedding. Even with his patronage, we met with no more friendliness than we expected. This disturbed us not, for we didn't go to the wedding in hopes of forging neighborly bonds. Nor did we go, as some later claimed, in order to watch the portioning of the guest gelt, though knowing who got what did turn out to be useful. We attended the wedding simply to see if we might do something for Thord's former wife Aud.

Despite her garb, Aud was not really what I'd call mannish. Still, she was a strong-headed woman. Thord's kinfolk thought so, too. Bracing themselves for retaliation, they patrolled the wedding hall heavily armed. They needn't have worried. Aud's kinsmen had not the same fiber as Aud herself. Rather than crashing Thord's wedding and smashing everything up, they contented themselves by sulking at home.

The next day, we visited Aud. She retained us.

It would take us a few weeks to get things ready, but we agreed that the delay worked in everyone's favor. By the time we raised a ritual platform, the two most powerful men at the wedding, one a kinsman of Gudrun and the other the district chief, would be sailing for the conquering land of Denmark.

We had barely knocked the platform together when Aud took matters into her own hands. She rode to Thord's farmhouse at night, taking only a thrall for company. While the boy held her horse, she burst into the house and slashed open her former husband's chest. The knife cut so wide and deep, it was doubted for a few months that Thord would regain use of his arms.

Such a woman has no need of sorcery. She never paid us a thing. That's when it helped to know who got the most guest gelt.

SEASON OF SUMMER SOLSTICE

AT THE SUMMER market, Thord bruised my ribs with a kick, stinting even a scrap of his wares. I cared not. I wasn't after his withered apples and mold-raddled cheese. I slinked back to his stall, lingering just out of reach, to eavesdrop on the quarrel between him and his new wife Gudrun.

The basis was thus. Thord's mother Rigmor had sent them a message claiming that our proximity had become unbearable. Thord must come and get her, and her things, so she could live in his household.

No one could deny that her guest gelt had been stolen before she spent even a pfennig of it. We agreed, though, that her complaint was mainly a ploy to get what she had long craved: a hearth less lonely than her own. Her cottage perched on a spit of land accessible only by sea or by an arduous trip through a waste-land riddled with potholes, some of which might suddenly erupt, drenching horses and people with scalding mud.

Most people considered Rigmor meddlesome and over-talk-ative, but Thord was ready to agree to her request. After all, it would be the women who mostly put up with her. For that same reason, Gudrun didn't take such a generous view on her mother-in-law sharing her household. She swore, in fact, she would put a wide floor between her own bed and Thord's, if Rigmor moved in. Let her go to Thord's sister, she said.

Thord pointed out what they both already knew, that Rigmor would not live with her daughter, whom she considered lazy and quarrelsome.

Then let her stay where she is, Gudrun said. She claimed that Rigmor lived comfortably, draining Thord's coffers—the sister put in not a pfennig—and over-indulging her servant. This was a mute and lame girl Thord had passed on as of no use to his own house-hold. Not to mention the guest gelt Rigmor got at the wedding.

I don't know why Gudrun added that. Rigmor's message stated clearly that we'd stolen all of it.

Gudrun said that, anyway, Rigmor's cottage lay little more than a stone's throw away. True enough, when the wind lay still they could see each other's cooking smoke. Yet while most of Thord's neighbors lived within a short ride, the holding he'd nicked out for his mother, as I said, lay on an awkward patch more easily reached by boat than horseback, and neither the old woman nor the maid-en could handle a boat. We were her nearest neighbors, and even so we had to stand on our roof to see her house from ours.

At our hearthside that night, we agreed that Rigmor had put Thord in a bind. His closed-handedness had eroded the status he'd inherited from his father. The way Gudrun had managed his di-vorce from Aud didn't help. He had hoped to reverse this decline with the wedding's guest gelt. Then he let Aud get away with cutting him, and his prestige fell still more. If it became known that he turned away his own mother, it could not get lower.

Thord and Gudrun cared not that the mother had been robbed of what was to them a paltry bag of gelt and to her a small fortune. Nor did they pause to consider the terror of an elder, living alone on a remote holding, robbed even as she lay in her own bed. She'd awakened, unfortunately, while I took hold of the gelt. On discussing the incident later, we agreed I had not been clumsy. The problem was, her bed stood against the wall, and she'd tucked the gelt well under her mattress.

In short, however they wanted to see it, Gudrun and Thord knew that refusing Rigmor's request would put them in a bad light. He would be seen as a poor protector and, worse, in thrall to his wife. Gudrun would be shunned as too heartless to carry out the most basic duty of a kinswoman. Whether Gudrun dragged her bed across the room or across the great hall, Thord had no choice but to bring his mother home.

He could have left it at that, but thinking to enhance his prestige, he decided to do something about us as well.

Being wealthy, though notoriously stingy, Thord had no trouble rounding up a dozen or so supporters—hard-pressed, all—to visit us. He didn't tell them, I guess, that they would also have to help move his mother's household. On arriving at Rigmor's cottage, Thord ordered most of them to crate and haul everything to his boat. He and a few chosen friends then rode to our holding.

At the time, we knew nothing of Thord's plans, either to move his old mother to his holding that day or to ride against us. All we knew was what I'd gleaned at market, that Rigmor wanted to live with Thord, and that neither he nor Gudrun wanted her to move in. We learned everything else later. Had we known that day what

Thord had in mind, Sulgrinn and I would have stayed home. Instead, we went to a hot spring where we liked to bathe.

Dad had just come back from the pasture when Thord and his companions galloped into view. Mother was tending our garden out front.

We were proud of the bounty Mother's care had raised from the little patch, though it were only herbs and simples, leathery greens and leeks, and some shy flowers. A wattle fence sheltered it from the wind, and old seaweed and horse manure had broken the surly clods into yielding soil.

Thord and his four men smashed right through the windbreak and milled about, their horses kicking and crushing. Dad and Mother deemed it wise to suppress their stately bearing, and assumed cringing meekness.

We later agreed that at the exact time Thord arrived, Sulgrinn and I were about halfway to our spring. He suddenly stopped. We must get home, he said. I turned back without question, for Sulgrinn's name as keen-eyed had not been idly given. By the time we arrived home, though, Thord and his gang were gone.

After destroying our humble dab of paradise, Mother and Dad told us, Thord stood in his stirrups and loudly issued us a summons to the þing, to answer accusations of theft and sorcery. Dad and Mother responded with quiet words and nods. Thord repeated the summons, probably hoping, Dad wryly observed, to evoke tears or wrath. They reaped only more nods. Finally, they left.

Mother and Dad did not bother to fix the garden, knowing full well that soon even Steini the Priest would no longer tolerate our presence.

The destruction of the garden incensed my brother and me, but the accusations laid against us stoked our anger to a white-hot blaze. No one had ever been so audacious as to throw us an open challenge. It didn't take us long to agree on a course of action, nor much longer to build a ritual platform, for we had prepared the lumber for it when we thought we would do something for Aud. When Sulgrinn saw that Thord and his companions had put out to sea, we mounted the platform and began singing potent incantations.

Magic first rises with a sense of extreme heaviness. Though the weight is but a trick, a stout and secure platform underfoot helps you through it. Then comes an urge to release water, much the way a sea-drowned man drains from his mouth and ears and everywhere else. Then a gnarled, turgid wind tosses your limbs. Then a fire hotter even than a smith's forge spirals into and out of you, burning all in its path, though it consumes not a thing. Finally, the spell catches, and everything happens at once. If you didn't piss yourself on the first round, you will by the time the magic's finished thrashing you.

In the gloaming of summer twilight, the sea began to lash and surge. Only Sulgrinn could see it from our platform, but the ecstasy of its savage and obedient sway moved us all. Higher and higher, our voices and hands plucked waves and wove winds.

The people watching from the shore to which Thord strove would later praise his courage and seamanship. He and his crew did show a desperate will to live. Over the gunwales went everything, from the equipage to the household goods Rigmor had packed so carefully, kettle to quilt, the crockery swaddled in moss as if it were Roman glass, as the neighbors learned from salvaging the flotsam. The crew did cruelly drive the horses leaping into the wrath-foamed tide.

The boat passed the worst reefs. She nearly made it in. Then Thord or his helmsman mishandled her and she broached to.

Many claimed that our last breaker drove her onto the rocks. Keen-eyed Sulgrinn saw it: poor seamanship wrecked that boat.

It was too bad that Rigmor and her girl had to pay the price for Thord's arrogance.

SEASON OF THE AUTUMN EQUINOX

THE NEIGHBORS FEARED Steini the Priest as much they feared us, as I learned dogging around the market the following week. Even after the bloated bodies of Thord and his companions, including his old mother and the maiden, washed onto the land, people made one excuse after another to avoid confronting Steini about us. Maybe the rich salvage, together with memories of Thord's high-handedness and stinginess, calmed their outrage.

Who could say for sure, they pondered, if the storm was maliciously wrought or merely a freak of weather? And poor Rigmor could no longer testify about the robbery. Anyway—not to speak ill of the dead—she always had been one to exaggerate things. And—again not to speak ill of the dead—everyone knew Thord had treated his mother shamefully. If his kin defamed us, well, it was only natural they would try to shift the blame away from him. Some complained when we did not attend the þing, but no one came to arrest us. Steini himself we placated with twisty words and a particular herbal tea that Mother blended. We shared with him some coin as well, though being a generous man he never demanded tithe or rent. He never asked, either, how we got more local coin than our wares earned at the market.

What mostly kept us safe, though, was the absence of three people who had more drive than their slack-sinewed neighbors. Gudrun had loved Thord, despite their incessant quarreling, and she lacked neither courage, intelligence, and resoluteness, nor powerful allies, not least of whom was her kinsman Gwennhael, who held power and prestige second only to the district chief Jofurr. However, she lay abed at her parents' holding, suffering a difficult pregnancy not helped by her husband's death. As for Gwennhael and Jofurr, they had not yet returned from Denmark, where they had sailed shortly after the wedding. When these three—Gudrun, Gwennhael, and Jofurr—were ready to attend to recent events, our time in the district would be up.

On the first day clear enough for travel, Dad set off on our black stallion, a spirited animal only he could mount. A strong man named Toki lived outside the western edge of the district, about a day's ride from us. This Toki had an eye for fine fighting horses and a compulsion to own them, and we had hopes that he would agree to protect us in exchange for the stallion. Meanwhile, Mother, Sulgrinn, and I paid a call to Steini the Priest, with the goal of gaining time enough, before we had to leave the neighborhood, to glean a bit more of that guest gelt, for Toki was known as a greedy man who loved gold as much as horses.

Snow crusted the ground, and the air, brittle as glass, made little stabs within my chest with every breath. We saw, as we approached Steini's house, a thrall leading a pony and a horse to the barn. I recognized the boy, for at the market I had often tagged behind his master, none other than Gudrun's kinsman, Gwennhael.

I'd been unhappy when Gwennhael left for Denmark. Doglike, I'd grown attached to him. I was more unhappy to see him returned sooner than expected, and yet more unhappy to find him at Steini's. Only urgent business would bring him here when his ship would barely have weighed anchor. It was easy to guess what that business was.

We wondered if we should turn back, then decided Gwennhael wasn't the type to attack another man's guests, and we unarmed at that. Mother added, we were unlikely to get the chance to say anything for ourselves, but if we kept quiet we would leave knowing more than we had on arriving. So we went on in.

Steini greeted us with friendliness, but his manner was strained. Gwennhael treated us with courtesy that lacked any warmth. We had been wise to plan the end of our stay here. If on his part Gwennhael was dismayed to see us, whom clearly he had come to speak against, he did not show it any more than I did betray the feelings that the sight of him raised in me. This was by no means the first time I had met in man form someone I knew only in dog form. Never before, though, had I spent time in man form with someone under whose glamour I'd fallen as a dog.

Steini, tactfully, did not delay the proceedings beyond offering mulled cider and some cake. Gwennhael, after his cold greeting, addressed only the Priest, speaking of us as if we were not sitting right there.

Sulgrinn, as quick to anger as he was to merriment, plainly found his manner insulting. Mother's placid mien contained his wrath.

I endured. Besides Gwennhael's glamour, another thing made it difficult for me, and me only. Throughout his visit, regardless of the fact that he never spoke to us, save with the briefest words courtesy demanded, Gwennhael flicked me with glances, very quick, yet very penetrating. I did my best not to catch his eye, even as I could not resist stealing glances at him. It was my dog's heart compelling me, we agreed later, and maybe it compelled Gwennhael as well, for the glamour between man and dog is nearly always bothfelt. It is a most cunning kind of magic, too, for part of its working is to rob its subjects of the wish to throw it off, whatever they might suffer for it.

Gwennhael said to Steini, I've received complaints that your tenants have been making trouble in the district. My kinswoman Gudrun, backed up by several others, informed me that her deceased husband personally issued them a summons to the þing, on charges of theft and sorcery.

Steini responded in roundabout terms, implying that Gudrun's spite was goaded by grief and perhaps shame over neglecting her husband's mother. Figuring Gwennhael would get around to the tempest, he added, everyone knew that at this time of year, the sea could be impetuous—

Gwennhael cut Steini off with a polite gesture. He had not ridden out here, while his ship rode at anchor half-unloaded, to indulge in gossip. He came only to deliver a simple warning. We had not attended the þing, nor sent a proxy or any excuse. Thus, given the gravity of the charges and the overall situation, the general inclination in the district was to put us to death.

This news came as a shock, for I had heard nothing of it at the market only the week before. Gudrun must have risen from her childbed with a vengeance, to turn opinion against us so quickly. Sulgrinn flushed dark, but Mother's subtle gesture, together with her radiant composure, again subdued him. This was just as well, for Steini's skillful negotiation won us our lives.

Ultimately Gwennhael promised Steini we would not be pursued if we left the district tomorrow.

As soon as those terms were reached, Gwennhael rose, bade us all farewell, and departed. He left behind no doubt that he would keep his word.

We later agreed, with some humor, that Steini's wrath, expressed after the meeting, fell on us not so much for anything we'd done, but for having gotten him in bad with Gwennhael. Death was no less than we deserved, Steini swore, and only his duty as host had prompted him to intercede for us. We thanked him and vowed to keep the terms, not least because defying Gwennhael meant defying the whole district.

Thord's raid on our little holding had weakened our comfort in it. Still we left the next day with little cheer. Three times before, the force of evil rumors had driven us from our abode. We had learned the hard way, too, that simple contentment raises envy higher even than heaps of gold. This time, at least, we did not face a long and treacherous voyage over the sea, as we had the second time.

We headed west on our three fine horses, hoping that when we met Dad on the road he would bear good news. Around midday Sulgrinn spotted him, and we picked up our pace that we might meet sooner.

Once we were all together again, our journey fell into a more comfortable rhythm. Dad shared news both good and bad.

Toki had agreed to take us in, though he drove a mighty hard bargain. When Dad asked his protection in return for the stallion, Toki laughed and said it was a poor trade, even for such a fine animal, given that the whole district buzzed with rumors against us. Dad assured him that Gudrun, who had spread the slander, could hardly be trusted, given the way she'd tricked her first husband into divorce, and wronged Thord's first wife, too. This was a skillful thrust on Dad's part, for Gudrun had once rejected Toki, and he relished any words against her. Dad pressed his advantage by telling Toki that another man wanted the stallion, but Dad was reluctant to let him have it, since he was likely to try and put him to the plough. Toki agreed that the man in question was a milk-liver who never put his horses up to fight, unlike himself, who regularly put his best horses to the test. Dad commented that given his fighting spirit, a family under his protection would not be at the mercy of jealous and scheming neighbors.

Toki gave in, with the promise of the stallion—plus coin, which, of course, we didn't have to spend, not daring yet to trade with Rigmor's guest gelt. We would have to give up all four of our horses. This was too bad, especially since Mother was fond of her little mare, but it couldn't be helped.

Dad had further news, which turned out to be more interesting than he expected. Not only did Toki's and Gwennhael's holdings adjoin each other, but the two men were half-brothers. Toki's manner in referring to Gwennhael had made it clear to Dad that the two men didn't get along. After some discussion, we agreed that these ties worked to our advantage. Living on Toki's holding would put us in close proximity to Gwennhael, but as long as we didn't violate our terms Gwennhael would have nothing to say about it. Moreover, Gwennhael wasn't the type to cross another man's honor, let alone his own half-brother's, even if they did hold little love for each other. Thus, Toki's protection would, in a sense, also bind Gwennhael.

I added what I had heard about Gwennhael, when I'd gone about as a dog in the market. His influence, I'd gathered, drew not only from a wide network of kinsmen and contacts, but from a rare alloy of generosity, physical strength and courage, courtesy, and a charisma utterly lacking in arrogance. Moreover, he possessed a particular talent for sensing the undercurrents of a situation. The district chief Jofurr considered Gwennhael honest and reliable, both in advice and in deed. Taking all that into account, we had been wise not to go against him.

I hadn't yet mentioned the warmth I'd felt sitting near Gwennhael, a warmth that had nothing to do with Steini's generous hearth. Still, Dad, Mother and Sulgrinn knew I had more to say, and that I would come out with it in my own time. And so we went on quietly, while I turned some thoughts in my mind.

When Sulgrinn was nearly a man, he had told us he might enjoy fucking with men, though at the time he had not yet tried it. I myself have ever craved sex only with women. Nevertheless, I couldn't deny an intense pull to Gwennhael, and his physical glamour was part of it.

When I finally came out with these thoughts, we did enjoy a good laugh, that I, not Sulgrinn, would be the one seduced by Gwennhael. Dad said that given Gwennhael's fame, the same thing must happen to many other men, and many women, too.

And many dogs, too, Sulgrinn teased.

Just as I like to take dog form, Sulgrinn's truths like to take joke form. He had noticed the glances Gwennhael gave me during the visit, and wondered if Gwennhael might have found me familiar, without, of course, knowing me as the dog that tagged after him at market. We agreed this was much more likely than the possibility that Gwennhael had cast a spell over me. Still, Mother suggested we do a ritual, just in case, after we reached our new home.

The conversation had taken on a somewhat light-hearted mood, but eventually grim exile silenced us. Nostalgia for our old country over the sea mingled with the reality that we had again been cruelly cast out.

As dusk crept over the land, it brought to me not its usual comfort, but a sense that I was not in myself, but rather watching myself riding along. I didn't mention this aloud. The rising moon finally displaced the uncertain gloaming, and the feeling dispersed, even as thoughts of Gwennhael came over me again, growing more and more vivid to my inner vision.

We sat in a warm room, he a man and I a dog. He glanced at me, just as I lifted my head to look at him. Our eyes locked—and he knew who I was.

The next thing I knew, I lay sprawled on the ground. Worse, Mother, Dad, and Sulgrinn had ridden on—they hadn't noticed me fall! My horse, luckily, stayed near, and at her friendly nudge, I mounted and soon caught up with my family.

Small as it seemed—I fell asleep and took a tumble, with only a bump on my head and a bruised hip to show for it—the incident upset and disturbed us. No one needed point out its ominous cast. By mutual consent we spoke no more of it, for too much talk on one topic, as Dad often said, can be as potent as incantations.

The terrain did nothing to lift our gloom. This part of the district had an especially desolate and hostile mien. Never well settled yet heavily logged, swathes of rotting stumps and moss spread where once stood deep forests of majestic firs. Creeping mists alive with moonlight, usually a source of enjoyment and even revelry for us, seemed to twine our horses' legs with malignant intent.

Glad we were when through the clinging fog wafted the homey spice of turf smoke from Toki's holding. Yet we did pass by the hump of his dwelling, preferring to go on to the cottage given us, cold and dark as it was.

・・・

SULGRINN HAD BITTERLY denounced Steini the Priest for making us leave. He might even have cursed him, had Mother permitted. Not long after we settled in our new home, though, we came to agree: Steini was an honorable man who had done his best for us in a sticky situation.

Toki was another kind of person. He priced his protection not by friendship and mutual respect but by bribery and flattery, and his power in the locality lay not in true prowess and generosity, but in a willingness to bully and exploit his neighbors. As the months passed, it became clear that, once more, it was only a matter of time before those neighbors turned on us. Then Toki, in turn, would betray us in some fashion.

Some news I gathered while dogging around the market confirmed our cares. A priest named Snorri—the same we'd warded from Steini's parish—had lately visited Gudrun. When Gudrun confided to this Snorri her unslaked wish to avenge the death of her husband, he counseled her to bide her time. Toki would do the job for her, he said, and in the bargain he would get his due for harboring us in the first place.

We did not doubt the priest's insight, even as the season trapped us. When winter draws close, people draw in and grow more unwilling to aid strangers. In short, we found ourselves stuck between an unreliable protector and poor prospects elsewhere. On those premises, we made a fatal mistake.

Toki had formed a habit of dropping in at our cottage, especially after Dad's beer finished fermenting and was deliciously flavored with Mother's herbs. We did not enjoy his company, but he was our patron. Besides, we counted on him to trade for us at the market, even if the provisions he brought us in exchange for our goods were far inferior in value.

On a visit early in the season of the sun-waning, he boastingly described his encounter with a man from a big farm adjoining his own holding. This man, named Elden, was a head taller and much hairier than Toki, but the two of them held a few traits in common. They both were known far and wide as vain bullies, and they both loved fine horses.

According to Toki, Elden swaggered up to the stall where Toki sold, among his own meager goods, our beer and some yarn Mother had dyed in really beautiful colors, including a pure leaf-green no other artist could attain. I happened to be there, as a dog, and can attest that Toki gave a fairly accurate account of his meeting with Elden.

Toki initiated their conversation, saying, I've heard you're no coward, Elden of Bjorgarfjord.

His gambit may sound like admiration, but it was intended to provoke. Not only did Toki probe Elden's mettle, he deliberately insulted Elden's vanity, for the big man preferred to be known as Elden of Eldenstead, his own large and prosperous holding.

Elden did not take the bait, for he had business to do. He told Toki he had come to buy the black stallion he got from the witch man, meaning Dad.

Toki bluntly told him the stallion was not for sale.

Elden seemed to think Toki was haggling and offered to trade four stud horses and so much more gelt besides, the neighbors would call Toki the cleverest huckster in the world.

Toki didn't intend to sell the stallion at any price, but Elden's words were particularly ill-chosen, for the whole district knew that only Toki's kinship with Gwennhael saved him from having to face the þing for crafty dealings.

I'm no huckster, Toki said, his face turning red, and that horse is not for sale. He added, even if the stallion were for sale, Elden would not get him for any price.

Elden responded by letting Toki know that he was more full of himself than he had a right to be. He followed up with a curse: I hope you'll be forced to sell that stallion, he said, for a far less generous price than I've offered.

This curse of Elden's, though of the kind thrown by people who have no magic, only threats, did end up fulfilling itself. Not that it did Elden himself a bit of good.

By now, a crowd had gathered. Gwennhael came to see what was happening, with the clear intention to intervene if things got further out of hand. His presence only provoked Toki to show off.

Step up, Toki challenged Elden, and let's see if you can bully me out of those horses.

Instead of stepping up, Elden stepped back, drawing a laugh from the crowd. You think you're hot shit, he blustered, but by the end of the summer I'll come take a look at those fine animals, and we'll see whose barn houses them this winter.

Sure, Toki replied. Come on over. Just be ready to fight fair.

After Elden left and the crowd dispersed, Gwennhael advised Toki to go carefully, for Elden was likely to make good on his threat.

We thought his advice uncharacteristically foolish, not by a lack of sense, but in that he bothered to give it at all. Predictably, Toki retorted he could tend his own affairs and Gwennhael had better keep out of them. His reply was all the hotter due to the settled opinion in the district that Gwennhael cast him in the shade.

Reflecting on the incident, we agreed that Toki's temper made him more enemies than friends, and his protection would do nothing to improve our situation in the district. On the other hand, nearly everyone esteemed his half-brother. I suggested attaching myself, as a dog, to Gwennhael's household. His hearthside could not be equaled for keeping track of the neighbors' business, and if we lived quietly over the winter and helped people in subtle ways, according to the problems they laid out to him, our fortune might recover at least enough to keep us safe at home.

That decision, I ardently regret. But Fate is a trickster who likes to unfold our mistakes too late for remedy.

Shifting form is arduous magic, but from then on I visited Gwennhael's holding almost daily, helping herd the sheep and geese and making sure I got along with the other dogs and the horses. Gwennhael assumed I was a puppy from one of Toki's dogs, for his half-brother allowed his animals to roam all over, regardless of boundaries. Indeed, one of Gwennhael's studs bore fresh scars from an ungoverned fight with the stallion Toki got from us.

I was encouraged by how well-treated I was by kin, hired help, and thralls alike. Gwennhael's twelve-year-old son Lambi grew especially fond of me, and we rambled about together for days long. The boy was Gwennhael's favorite, and I could see why. Lambi was strong, lively, bold, and kind-hearted. I soon grew as attached to him as he did to me, for a dog's nature goes deep, even when its form is a mere shift. The boy's love passed to me his father's favor as well, and I was let inside the house to loll and play with Lambi at the hearth.

Sometimes Gwennhael joined us in our frolics. Or he might doze in his fireside chair as we wrestled or cuddled up at the hearth. Sulgrinn teased me about the pleasure I found at Gwennhael's feet.

Mother and Dad advised me to be careful, for a dog's heart is made to be broken, being both unwaveringly loyal and ever astray.

I did not heed their warnings.

How could I have known the depth of sorrow that my dog's heart would bring on us all?

SEASON OF WINTER SOLSTICE

ONE CHILL MORNING, I was tagging along with one of Gwennhael's thralls when we saw Elden at the lower pasture. He did not see us, intent as he was on rounding up Toki's horses, which had wandered there. These horses included the black stallion and the three others that had been ours. The thrall didn't recognize Elden. He only knew Elden wasn't one of Toki's men, for Toki wouldn't bother to send anyone to get his horses off other people's pastures. The thrall hurried back to the farmhouse, with me at his heels, to report the situation to his master.

Once the thrall described the trespasser, Gwennhael assessed the situation immediately, not without irritation. He had no wish to get involved in Toki's quarrels. Besides, as he grumbled to his wife, who had just set a mug of hot ale before him, he didn't care for Toki's habit of letting his animals roam wherever they wished. Including his hounds, he said, pulling my ears affectionately. Nevertheless, kin being kin, he threw over his drawers and nightshirt a wolf fur gotten in some long-ago foreign campaign, grabbed an old but well-honed battle ax, and went to confront Elden.

The only sign of Gwennhael's age, besides a sprawling household and a well-weathered complexion, was a limp leftover from an old battle injury. Still, though we left the house on foot, we easily caught up with the horse thief, for the lower pasture spread not far from the farmhouse.

Gwennhael greeted Elden with a facetious semblance of

courtesy. Where do you think you're taking those horses, Elden of Eldenstead? he asked.

Elden, armed and armored to the teeth, wearing a helmet and a coat of mail, and bearing shield, sword, and spear, grinned defiance at Gwennhael, who carried only a beat up ax and whose breast was protected only by a balding wolfskin. I'm keeping the promise I made to your brother, said he. I'm fetching the horses alone, with no companions.

Gwennhael could only laugh. Sneaking around, he said, while Toki's asleep in bed is hardly in keeping with your agreement. The least you can do is meet him face to face as you steal his horses.

Predictably, Elden flared up. Then go on and fetch him, you old fucker, he said. He even shook his spear in Gwennhael's face.

Given his gimpy leg, Gwennhael wasn't about to trek to Toki's holding to tattle on Elden. However, like most men of prowess, he preferred to resolve things peacefully, or at least to try. He offered Elden some of his own horses in exchange for releasing Toki's hors-es, though admittedly his weren't as valuable.

Again, predictably, Elden responded with bullying heat. If you think you can bribe or threaten me into giving up these horses, said he, you're wrong. He couldn't resist adding that, the horses now being his own, just like their previous owner he would not give them up for anything.

It was to be his last witticism. Gwennhael let him finish string-ing the horses together, then calmly hurled the battle ax at him. The blade bit clear through Elden's mail, clove his heart-bone, and sliced his heart in two. Needless to say, Elden promptly fell dead.

Gwennhael tossed stones over the body to keep off foxes and gulls. He then rode Elden's horse to Toki's holding, bringing along the horses on the string Elden had attached. I followed on foot.

I slinked under a bench in Toki's dooryard, not to chance someone vowing that I was not one of Toki's dogs, as Gwennhael believed. As I licked my sore paws, I listened to the exchange between the two half-brothers. It was brief.

Rather than express gratitude for the return of his horses, Toki accused Gwennhael of seeking glory at his expense. No good would come of it, Toki warned.

Gwennhael turned away, shaking his head in disgust. He did let me ride back to his holding on his lap, and maybe my affection soothed his spirit somewhat.

Lambi met us at Gwennhael's gate and insisted I go with him to round up the sheep. Then we played tug the rope until nearly dusk.

I arrived home to learn that Toki had left not long before, stuffed with Mother's stew and inebriated from repeatedly filling his mug with Dad's beer. Whatever blustering tale he might have made of the morning's events, the bare fact was that Gwennhael, wearing only drawers, a nightshirt, and an ancient wolfskin, had killed with one stroke of a rusty ax Toki's much younger and well-armed enemy. Toki saw only one result: when Gwennhael's prestige rose, his own would sink. Being a man reluctant to take care of his own business, for all his pride, he had decided we would be the ones to solve his problem. He wanted us to do something to humiliate Gwennhael.

Despite Toki's impatience, Mother, Dad, and Sulgrinn had put him off, not willing to agree to anything while I was gone. We talked it over for a long time.

I said I didn't like it. Gwennhael's deed deserved thanks, not punishment. And it wasn't as if Gwennhael had not tried to resolve the situation without violence, though true, Toki didn't know that, Gwennhael not having deigned to explain it. I then mentioned the various ways Gwennhael showed his superior nature, most of all in treating people with discretion and respect, while not losing any of his authority.

No one disagreed, but Sulgrinn teased that my dog nature

might be getting the upper hand. His joke had a truth-edge none of us could miss.

I made the point that in terms of loyalty, ours would be better paid to Gwennhael than to Toki, who would surely betray us, sooner or later. In fact, it was now clear that Toki had taken us on to bother Gwennhael. On the other hand, if we stuck to ordinary work and kept the law, we might gain a better situation, namely Gwennhael's protection.

Gwennhael will never take us under his protection, Dad said quietly, for the very reason we wanted his protection: he was not a man to go back on his word. That would include his terms with Steini, which he would also have made with the district chief Jofurr. On the other hand, he would not go against Toki, however much ill will lay between them. Thus, as long as we live quietly, he said, and keep Toki happy, we're safe here. Mother added that after the winter storms passed, we might even return home. It was just a dream, but it cheered us a little.

The truth was, we had no choice. It was too late in the season to seek another situation. Besides, Toki hadn't asked us to harm Gwennhael.

We all agreed we must placate Toki, we turned to the problem he'd put to us: how to embarrass Gwennhael without making serious trouble. Sulgrinn gleefully rubbed his hands together, and we couldn't help laughing. It figured he would be the one to find a way, for he was our chief of pranks and jokes.

As we know, Sulgrinn said, on the day people here call Yule, Toki will throw a feast at the assembly he built this summer.

I had heard little else at market this last month, for Toki's assembly hall, by design, outdid every other in the district. Tall enough for giants, through its gaudy-painted doorway three men could ride abreast. The wasteland of tree stumps not far from Toki's house bore dismal testimony to his grand hall.

We'll cast a spell, Sulgrinn said, that will keep Gwennhael's household cooped up in their farmhouse for the whole of Yule night. No harm will come to them. They will just be stuck at home in all their finery, their gifts going to waste.

Dad thought the plan had merit. Not only would Toki be spared his brother's presence, he could also imply to everyone that Gwennhael decided to skip the feast to save himself the cost of gifts and spare himself the truth of being outdone.

Being hardly more than a childish prank, Sulgrinn added, it would not bring Gwennhael's full wrath upon us.

The plan seemed to carry less risk than exciting Toki's animosity by refusing his request. Still, I couldn't rest easy. The spell we planned to use was supposed to have a gentle hold. Yet it would have to be strong enough to keep Gwennhael's large household inside, for everyone, kin and thralls, would be inside the farmhouse all day making ready for the feast. A small mistake on our part could have big results.

I silently made up my mind to warn Gwennhael in some way that would not spoil the plan but would safeguard his household against any harm worse than being a laughing stock for a few days. It was not a decision lightly made. Never before had I kept my thoughts hidden from my parents and brother. I sensed my secret would change our fate forever, yet I kept steady with it.

I have many things to regret, but for more than one reason, I will never regret that.

I soon found a means to carry out my plan. A young milkmaid had lately caught my eye. She was called Krobahn, a name evocative of our homeland, where it meant "white-handed." She did indeed have white hands, and very soft they were, from petting the sheep and milking them. This Krobahn, I enticed into a dalliance.

Oh, what bliss to lay with her, on the fragrant, springing grass mounded in the loft of the barn, the ewes bleating contentedly below, her hands ever so soft upon the different parts of me, and my hands upon the soft parts of her. Never had I fallen so deeply under the spell of a woman. When we were apart I often found myself lost in dreams of her body stretched and trembling against mine. Still, I took care not to forget what I needed her to know.

One twilight, a week or so before Yule, as Krobahn and I emerged from the sleepy languor of our coupling, I mentioned, as if in boast, that where I came from people could be confined by song, and no harm came of it—unless someone were so foolish as to try to break through the net of the spell. I then sang just a tiny bit of the spell, for her to know the sound of it.

She blinked, spellbound herself for a few moments, then asked what kind of country had such songs.

I told her of our home, where winter and summer hardly change places, with ice and snow unknown. I told her what her name means in my tongue, and she said in wonder that maybe we held our homeland in common, for though she remembered nothing of her parents, an old spinster of Gwennhael's once told her they had been considered foreign.

We dreamed of sailing together over the wild sea, Krobahn and I, to make our home where even the gustiest winds blow mild. I enchanted her with tales of our creatures: the big-eyed seals who play jokes on foolish sailors by taking on the guise of beautiful women; the tiny mice who plague the farmer but make cunning messengers for those canny enough to glean their squeaking chatter; the gleaming otters who love nothing more than to play with their pups in the rocky shallows; the mighty whales, chiefs of the deep. She did laugh at how much plant-eating we did, but quieted to a sigh when I uttered loving words to her in my native language. My heart ached with yearning for my lost home, and I half-believed the dreams I shared with this dear woman lying warm in my arms.

So all went well, and I felt assured that when the time came she would warn Gwennhael of the spell's powers, and he would keep his people safe inside the farmhouse.

· · ·

ON THE DAY called Yule, we packed food and drink, and bundled up well, for we would be outside for hours, keeping Gwennhael and his people within. We left our house at dusk, which fell a little after midday on this, the longest night of the year.

We kept off the main road, where we might meet folks traveling torch-lit. Instead, Sulgrinn guided us through Gwennhael's pastures. With no lanterns to betray us, we held tight to each other's belts. On passing the heap of stones under which Elden lay, we offered his ghost neither curse nor blessing.

Soon we reached the farmhouse. Its parchment-covered windows glowed bright. Quietly, we mounted the roof at the back corner, where the thatch nearly met the ground. After a few preparations, we began to sing.

The eaves of Gwennhael's house being deep, we could not see the doors and windows from the roof. We only knew that at some point, music struck up within, perhaps to drown our song. No one came out to challenge us, and I took ease that Krobahn had given Gwennhael my warning.

In the sleepiest depth of night, silence fell within. Soon after, considering our job done, we stopped singing, and stole off. We again used the low back corner of the roof to climb down. Thus we never saw what happened at Gwennhael's threshold only moments before we ended the spell.

· · ·

IN THE NEXT day's sluggish dawn, Sulgrinn discerned riders coming, well-armed and grim. We couldn't figure why several men, including Gwennhael as well as Jofurr himself, would want to rake us for a mere joke. Again, we did not yet know what had happened the night before. Sulgrinn could tell, however, that for some reason things had taken a very bad turn. We must flee, he said.

Without stopping even to gather provisions, we left the cottage and headed up into the mountains. Sulgrinn went ahead in hopes of finding a cave to conceal and shelter us.

He was captured first.

They bound him, I would learn later, covered his head with a coarse sack, and left him under the guard of a few men while the rest continued to hunt us.

After we realized Sulgrinn had been captured, our hope was to evade the hunt long enough to circle back and free him. Our chances dwindled, even as the feeble wintry sun dispersed the mists of dawn, for they went mounted. When Dad told me to take dog form as soon as we reached a quiet place, I knew he and Mother had given up their own chances.

Shifting is slow magic; time enough never came. The men brought us to bay at the edge of a crevasse filled with biting vapors.

Only when we were bound did we learn why they had coursed us so wrathfully. Gwennhael's voice broke, making the accusation: our spell had stricken his son Lambi dead.

The news that our song had killed my boy friend buckled my knees. Only Gwennhael's rough grasp kept me from falling to the ground. Though I was in man's form, the dog's heart twinned to my own forced from me a howl so piercing, one of the men quickly gagged me, thinking it a curse.

Mother and Dad pleaded for Sulgrinn's and my lives. None of the company heard them out, busy as they were gathering stones for the kill. I trembled and sobbed in Gwennhael's grip, not with fear, but with sorrow. I had betrayed my friend Gwennhael in the worst possible way, with Lambi slain by our spell. My beloved family's life would soon end. The thought that I would never again bury my face in my woman's hair and kiss her secret places doubled my sorrow. I blamed her not a bit for never having given, as I thought, the message that would have averted all this. How could I have asked that she, a mere thrall, dare tell a man like Gwennhael how to guard his family from a pretty song?

Suddenly Gwennhael's hands tightened on me so hard I would have screamed, had I not been gagged. He shouted, this one I sentence to outlawry!

Jofurr refrained from telling him that clemency did not lie in his power. He only ordered the men to pause in their grim harvest of stones. Given that Gwennhael was most deeply injured, he said, it was only justice to hear what he had to say.

Gwennhael repeated Krobahn's warning from the night before. Knowing that my beloved woman had given my message after all, and in such skillful terms, both comforted me and redoubled my anguish, that this brave and true woman would soon be forever parted from me.

For Gwennhael's sake, Jofurr agreed to sentence me to outlawry. I might rather have died alongside my parents on that day, but Mother's and Dad's tears said that my life gave them a last comfort. Besides, I could not give myself up to death without trying to save Sulgrinn, if he was even still alive. Nor could I give up Krobahn.

Most of the others, especially Toki, begrudged my life. When Jofurr did not change his mind, they said at least I should be forced to watch my parents fall bloodied and maimed under the hail of their stones. Despite the deep wrong he suffered, Gwennhael was not so cruel. He agreed with Jofurr that my term as outlaw started immediately. Later, I wondered if he recognized me, in some way, as the dog that so often rambled with him and his son, and dozed and tumbled with them at the fireside.

I hid myself until the killing was done and the men gone. They had covered the bodies, calling the pile of rocks the Devil's Cairn, an apt name considering the evil they had wreaked there. A son's devotion offered me no choice but to make sure nothing more could be done for my honored parents, yet I wish with all my heart I had not unpiled the cairn, and not only because of the fateful delay it caused. Sick to my core and blind with tears, I quickly heaped it up again. I then scrambled to where we'd guessed Sulgrinn was being held. I knew several shortcuts impossible to take by horse, but I arrived too late. The men had already descended the mountain. The last I saw of my brother, he rode bound and hooded in their midst toward the cold and endless sea.

The following I learned later, for at the time I could not catch up to their horses' brisk pace.

They did take my brother Sulgrinn down to the sea, where they launched a boat and put out for deep water. One of them jested to the effect that from the sea we came, and to the sea we would return, but Jofurr and Gwennhael cut off all such mockery and merriment. With somber mien, Gwennhael himself tied the heavy rock to my brother's neck with a strong rope.

My brother begged that he be allowed to lay eyes upon the land one last time. He claimed that my family hated the sea, as a cruel means of oblivion and exile, and we had loved life only with firm ground under our feet. His words carrying an element of truth, and this being Gwennhael's revenge, Jofurr looked to him. Gwennhael nodded, and Jofurr performed what he thought was a small mercy. He removed the hood from Sulgrinn's head.

Sulgrinn gazed toward the land of our exile—to be exact, at Toki's holding, though the men with him did not yet realize that. As Gwennhael himself later told, the look in his eyes was far from pleasant.

The day we came to this place, Sulgrinn said, was an unlucky one. He spoke slowly, as if making a rueful reflection on our life. In fact, he was gathering and directing a curse. He then said quickly, may Toki and his descendants never again find happiness.

Belatedly, the men tipped him over the gunwale, heaving the rock-weight after him. Sulgrinn quickly sank, and soon he drowned.

The curse of my beloved brother, whose bloated body drifted, tide by tide, back to this cursed shore, will certainly be very effective. Not only did it steal magic from over the threshold of death; the curse made by Sulgrinn, while he looked right at Toki's house, carried the force of justice.

Knowing as yet nothing of that, I found not a grain of comfort to sustain me over the long winter. I wandered, an outlaw, no better than a ghost, oft frozen to the bone, stealing shelter and provisions, warming myself, betimes, by setting ablaze a barn or wood hut when my grief and wrath grew too heavy to bear. I first drew out the animals, and they did come to me, running wild, their breath in panic steaming. These innocent ones were my only living company.

I longed to take dog form, that I might stretch out at some warm hearth with a friendly hand to tousle my ears. Yet I could not bear to do so, for it would recall too sharply the days when as a dog I played at Gwennhael's fireside with my boy friend Lambi. I feared it would not have protected me, anyway. Not from Gwennhael, at least.

In this wintry land populated by harsh men and the ghosts of my family, I dared not seek the comfort of Krobahn's embrace. She would be under watch for knowing about the spell, and I couldn't risk her life just to kindle my own spirits. But every night as she milked the ewes, she told me later, she kept her heart close to mine by singing the bit of song I'd sung to her. And she waited for spring.

SEASON OF SPRING EQUINOX

WITH THE HIGH pastures open on the mountain's flowered breast, Krobahn sang her shepherdess's spells with no one to hear but the sweet fleece-bearers—and me.

We made our marriage within her little hut, a square of stacked stone walls roofed with thatch and warmed by a low hearth. Our bed was a rough pallet perfumed with the grass and the flowers that filled it and with the scent of our two bodies entwined. When we could pull ourselves apart from each other, I taught her what I knew of my mother's ways of dying wool, and her special weaving patterns, and her herbal arts, for these crafts were rare and folks coveted their yield.

It was Krobahn who told me of my brother's end, having heard it from Gwennhael himself. Of Lambi, she said very little, knowing how badly I'd taken his death. Finally, one day when my courage was high, I asked her the question that had haunted me all winter. How did Lambi die that night? For as we both knew, we had directed no harm at anyone, let alone Gwennhael's favorite child, and she had warned Gwennhael, too.

Now the tragic story that she had kept locked within her came out.

When Gwennhael's household heard our singing, she said, they stopped everything they were doing and fell silent. It was as if they became dumb dolls. After her own first moments of bewilderment, Krobahn remembered what I had told her. As a mere thrall, she'd never spoken directly to Gwennhael. She also feared our love affair coming to light, for the district buzzed with Gudrun's slander against our family. Still, she plucked up her courage and approached him. She started by saying she'd heard a story from long ago about magic songs, or some such, but Gwennhael ordered her outright to say what she knew. Maybe he had already guessed something about her and me. She then told him the story we had agreed on, which went like this:

As she was bringing the milk from the barn that evening, the youngest one of the witches had appeared in the yard. She had met me before, and found me handsome and friendly, though she claimed that was as far as it went.

Gwennhael looked at her long and hard, then bade her continue.

As we chatted in the yard, she said, the witch told her that certain songs could weave magic nets around habitations. Even though these nets were generally harmless, no one should risk getting entangled in them. She pretended she thought my words only idle boasting, until the song began.

Krobahn withstood another long look from her master. Then, without questioning her further, Gwennhael gave his household stern orders that no one must go out or be let in.

Gwennhael barred the door and stationed the young men to guard the windows, then bade his household enjoy their own feast of Yule with music and feasting. This he did not only to assuage their harsh disappointment at missing the party in Toki's new assembly. Merrymaking would distract from our song, and temper the urge each felt to go outside.

This went wrong for a reason none of us could ever have foreseen. Krobahn herself never completely understood it, for I never confessed to her shifting into dog form.

As she told it, a few dogs happened to be inside when we began singing. Lambi worried that his dog, that is myself, might try to seek him and stumble into the spell. His father assured him that the spell did not affect dogs. This lie or mistake, I don't know which, did not calm the boy. Lambi's mother tried to divert him with some of the toys intended to have been given away at Toki's feast. Still, Lambi kept begging to call his dog in.

Evil tongues later wagged to the effect that our spell had been directed against the child. Such is the slander you face when forced to abide in a strange land. The unbearable possibility remains, though, that my voice in particular fretted Lambi.

After wandering with tear-wet face from door to window to window, Lambi finally joined the revelries. Krobahn later thought that his play was but a sham, and that he was really awaiting his chance to sneak out and find his dog.

Our singing, as I already knew, outlasted the party. One by one, despite Gwennhael's efforts, his people dropped to sleep. Even he himself succumbed.

With everyone slumbering but himself, Lambi opened the front door and stepped out. The chill draft woke Gwennhael, too late. Lambi lay dead not more than a few steps from the threshold.

Krobahn's account broke my heart anew, though I gulped into sobs the howls that climbed from my chest to my throat.

She tried to comfort me with the conviction that Gwennhael had willingly lent to my brother's last curse the strength of his own bitterness, for during the hunt for us, Toki had let slip that our spells had been at Toki's bidding.

Gwennhael's craving for vengeance festered until finally he went to Jofurr and asked permission to issue Toki a challenge. He didn't get the answer he wanted.

Jofurr was not about to allow a blood feud to pollute the entire neighborhood. He did state that Toki would eventually get his due. Gwennhael needed only be patient, as he ever had been in adversity.

Gwennhael persisted, driven by his own and his wife's grief. No longer could he abide with Toki. The evils of a blood feud notwithstanding, the district simply could not hold the two of them.

In considerate but no uncertain terms, Jofurr warned Gwenn-hael that to go against Toki was to go against Jofurr himself.

Gwennhael recognized that he had no choice but to back down. Once returned to his own hearth, he assured Lambi's mother that Jofurr subtly promised to take care of things with Toki.

Krobahn shared that belief, but I wasn't so sure. Gwennhael's claim that Jofurr himself would punish Toki rang more as an empty boast to soothe his wife and salvage his pride, bruised from having come home not with a challenge made but with the order that he must hold back his just wrath.

Krobahn and I spoke no more of the matter after that, preferring to live in an enchanted peace. Then one day she delivered news that tore me in two, between joy and grief.

I first filled her with my joy, even as the wisdom born of sorrow—that I would never in life see our child she carried in her womb—made clear: my death will serve a greater purpose than my own oblivion. In the dimmest hour of the night, we carefully laid out to each other the essential and entire truth of our situation.

Krobahn believed that Gwennhael did not seek my blood. Moreover, she said, the tide was turning, and people would come to agree with Gwennhael that Toki was entirely to blame for Lambi's death, and that we had been persecuted unjustly.

When she said, we, she included herself, counting herself as one with my family. This pierced my heart with both pride and sorrow. I kissed her, and we made love again, and finally continued our parley.

I conceded that Toki's neighbors did dislike him strongly for making trouble. But they considered us a large part of that trouble. And if Gwennhael avenged himself as he wished, Toki's kin would blame us for that as well.

Krobahn listened closely, for we both knew our child's life was at stake. Her strength and clear-sightedness gave me strength to bring out the truth that she and I had kept at bay, this blissful summer.

We need not concern ourselves with Toki, I said. Justice will visit him, drawn by the power of my brother's curse.

Drawing her close, I went on. I will live out my remaining days as an outlaw, I said. There is no choice in that matter. But my death can come by exposure or wild animals, or by the malice of men.

Here the tears started from my eyes, and from hers, mingling on our cheeks. And yet this was only the beginning of our sorrow, whose heaviest part my beloved woman was destined to bear.

I told her, we must choose the malice of men.

• • •

I CONTINUED TO make plenty of trouble in the neighborhood, and more than one farmer complained to Jofurr of my depredations. Slowly, I tightened my influence to Gwennhael's holding, for I knew he would be the one to get something done. His ewes yielded less and less milk, for I had laid a curse on them. Krobahn herself, of course, fell under suspicion, just as we planned. She revealed, on being questioned, that the handsome young witch had been visiting her and had given her some trinkets.

From this point, there was no going back.

She trembled and cried as she made her confession. It wasn't terror, as they thought, that shook her limbs and pushed the tears from her eyes. It was the force of the betrayal she must arrange. She did not let her emotions get the upper hand, though. She had to make things go our way without raising suspicion.

She had noticed some time ago that Jofurr gazed at her in a certain way, though being a prudent man he otherwise kept his desire to himself. She hinted that if she were free, she could go where she wished.

Jofurr could take that however he wanted. Gwennhael himself

wanted her gone, what with her dalliance with me. Both agreed to her terms: in exchange for her freedom, she would turn me over to the men. A young ram with a twisted horn acted as courier between us. When it came up to the hut, I knew the agreement had been made.

With the upper meadows browning, Krobahn had brought the flocks down to a lower pasture. I came to her there and we did embrace and kiss each other one last time. I then laid my head in her lap. She pretended to comb lice from my hair, and I pretended to fall asleep.

· · ·

I know my end will unfold just as Krobahn and I planned, on that long night up in our little stone hut. That certainty, together with the deep intimacy Krobahn and I share, permit me to continue to speak, in a way, after my death; that is, when Krobahn tells our tale to our child.

Now, here they come, the last words of my story.

· · ·

After Krobahn admits she is carrying my child, she'll ask to be sent home to her people. Not only will Jofurr let her go, he'll pay her passage. Like Gwennhael, he is not a cruel man. He also takes a realistic outlook on things and will face the fact that a child of mine would cause plenty of discord and trouble in the district. She knows, too, where we stashed the gelt, left behind on the day of our futile flight. We decided she should not risk using it herself, but would turn it over to Jofurr and get the reward for it.

While Krobahn waits out winter's storms before taking passage, a hellish blizzard of ice will destroy Toki's barn roof, ruining the provender within. He will be forced to sell his fighting horses, including the black stallion ill-gotten from us. This same storm will deliver my brother from the sea to the shore below Toki's holding. The neighbors will cover the body with stones, but Sulgrinn will make trouble, maybe in the form of a joke. In the shape of a cow, for example, he might challenge Toki's old dairyman to a fight. After that fright, no one will object to laying my brother's body to rest with my parents. Standing alone at the foot of the cairn, Steini the Priest will murmur a few words on their behalf to his god, also unjustly slain.

Jofurr will rid the district of Toki, exiling him over the sea after a thrall is found strangled in his barn. In a strange land, isolated and set to, Toki will remember well the curse my brother laid on him, and he'll wish with all his heart he had never crossed us. He may gather wealth, but he will never reap happiness, nor get the chance to struggle against old age. So much for Toki.

Krobahn and our child will make a good home far away, though it will be not in our homeland. Instead, they will settle in Norway, for a Norseman once told me, in that country the water lies as shining blue lakes filled by ribbons of water that tumble down the sides of tree-clad mountains. At the edge of one of these lakes, Krobahn's cottage will nestle. Her sheep will go about fat and thick-clad, and by a warm fire she will dye, spin, and weave. Blending my mother's craft with her own, she will robe a tall, strong queen. Our child will bring her comfort and happiness to the end of her days.

There, I lose the thread. I know not how well my descendants will go forth in this world.

•••

IN THE MEADOW, I stretched out with my head pillowed on my beloved woman's lap, my eyes closed as if lulled to sleep by her gentle hands. She then did what she had to do. She slipped away.

Soon Gwennhael and Jofurr and their men came for me and, in some manner, put me to death.

•••   •••

The Tibetan Deity of Wisdom

THE DAY BEFORE the Captain turned forty, she got ordered to a postal depot in Q— N— Province. The trip wasn't a birthday present from the Army. No one in the distribution area was getting mail, and her orders were to fix it. The carrier dropped her off, hovered until its engines stopped coughing, then bobbed away.

Billows of dust lay down. The Captain put a hand on her belly, burped, swallowed. The patches of sweat on her jacket joined each other.

Once a sprawling camp, the depot had shrunk to rotten asphalt, dirt paths, a jumble of board-and-batten shacks with rusty roofs, and a couple dozen enlisted men. The perimeter's barbed wire snagged trash and jungle vegetation poisoned by whatever the surplus market sold as herbicide.

Stagnant, like the rest of Earth, the wondrous Blue Marble an abandoned toy after the 1970s, when the Pentagon found a bigger, better habitable planet and a way to get there. Not that the Earth stopped turning. It turned and turned faithfully in place. Farmers farmed, factories manufactured, and good soldiers followed orders, though the Commander-in-Chief dispatched his whims from the other end of the galaxy.

The Captain lifted her cap, ran a hand through her hair. Once upon a time, in days of yore, she'd dreamed of being a sea captain sailing to adventures far from home. She'd for sure achieved the captain and the far-from-home parts.

A soldier emerged from a longish shack, probably a barracks. Despite Army regs, his hair straggled in something like dreadlocks over his shoulders. He was white, but he reminded the Captain of her son. Except the soldier didn't have tattoos covering his arms, and he was, literally, yellow. He didn't look like a drinker. Probably liver parasites. His wrists stuck out from his jacket sleeves.

"Did you have a good trip, ma'am?"

On a carrier that should have been scrapped thirty years ago.

"Soldier?"

"Yes, ma'am?"

"Where's your name patch?"

"I don't have one, ma'am."

"I see. Lead on, soldier."

The soldier's feet dragged and his back bent to the Captain's kit bag as if it held cinderblocks.

As they approached a cabin with a patched screen door, a man in BDU trousers and a singlet burst out, head down, a bunch of papers in his hands. He didn't look up or even pause, let alone greet a visiting officer. He scurried into a hut with a fly-curtain across the doorway. By tropical standards, he could be said to be bustling.

"Is that the Sergeant in command?" the Captain asked.

"Yes, ma'am." The yellow-skinned soldier leaned into the cabin and dropped the kit bag on the floor. He stood before her, waiting. He had about the most gentle face she'd ever looked upon.

"Thank you, soldier. That's all."

She stepped in the cabin. Thumbtacks riddled the walls, some pinning torn-off corners of paper. The Captain had to laugh. No wonder the Sergeant had been in such an almighty rush. Would he have ripped down the porn for a male officer? Probably. Just to be safe.

Whatever smut the walls had borne, they were clean. The cabin smelled pleasantly tart and oily, like old-fashioned furniture polish—which maybe it was. The table, the stool that served as a nightstand, even the plywood-paneled walls glowed. The cot legs were set in little bowls of water, clear glass with scalloped rims. No personal belongings in sight. Hard to reconcile a porn palace with such tranquil cleanliness.

A little scorpion scuttled from somewhere. The Captain lifted her foot to crush it, changed her mind, and booted the creature out the door more gently than it deserved. She allowed herself a gusty sigh and went out.

The road through camp mixed dust and dried mud. It would be a wallow when it rained. Snake and rodent holes laced the edges. The mess hall earned its name. The latrines… No man who valued his jewels would sit on or even squat over the stained, cracked wooden seats, and yet something reeked and gave feast to what hummed and buzzed below.

Other than its quietness—just a few motors, no music, no yelling—the depot could have been any number of posts the Captain had toured, during this and the first war. And would tour, no doubt, during the next war and the next. Like that old movie *Ground Hog Day*: come and gone and come again, except not a day but whole wars, come and gone and come again.

She poked her head in the barracks. Yellow-skin had returned to a card game, sitting cross-legged with his buddies on a few cots pushed together. The soldiers stared at the Captain, at each other. Finally, they made to get up, but the Captain left without seeing if any of them remembered to salute.

The post office, about the size of the cabin allotted her, had a real door, locked, with a window. The Captain peeked in. Heaps of mail covered the floor. Some envelopes were metered, many hand-written and stamped, with stick-on return labels decorated with birds, flowers, lighthouses, what have you.

Elaborate orders from headquarters jumped through unfathomable tracts of space in minutes. Earthside, the mail, made of paper, took days or even weeks. Months. Forever, from this particular depot.

The Captain turned away and stood on the top step, staring out. Beyond the barbed and wilted perimeter, the jungle's mass hugged soggy, green shadow.

As the Captain clomped down the steps, the Sergeant emerged from the fly-curtained hut. What had kept him in there while a visiting officer roamed about? A girl? Or a nap, judging by his sludgy eyes. Sludgy eye, rather. The left orb stared blank, blind, clean. Glass. And the Army retained him. And the jaundiced kid. Why not? Park the walking wounded at a mail depot far from the desultory front lines.

The Sergeant put one hand to the bill of his cap and pulled it forward, put the other hand to the back and gave it a tug. His cap settled, he drew himself up and saluted.

"Ma'am." His face was dark pink. The heat, she guessed, not a blush.

"Sergeant," the Captain said in her neutral officer's voice.

In the last war, she would have called a muster and reamed the man out, bawled out the whole lot of them. Set them to cleaning the latrines, the mess hall, the barracks. Scrub out the floor cracks with toothbrushes. She would have ordained that the long-haired be shorn and the bearded shaved. She might even have made them plant flowers, just for the hell of it.

She didn't do that shit anymore. She just wanted to get the job done.

"You know why I'm here, Sergeant?"

The Sergeant licked his lips. He might have been about to launch his excuse story, or he might have thought of trying: No, ma'am. But his good eye flicked to the post office and that left nothing to say except: "Yes, ma'am."

"Good. Have the mail sorted and on the pad ready to be loaded tomorrow at o-nine-hundred hours."

The carrier wasn't due until ten, but the Captain wasn't taking chances. Tight itinerary for the birthday girl tomorrow. 0900: Mail sorted and on the pad. 0915: Commanding Sergeant thoroughly versed in the importance of hauling the mail, sorted, to the pad every blessed week at o-nine-hundred hours. 1000: Depart, with mail, to main base. 1200: Extensions, manicure and pedicure. 1530: Busy work that won't fuck up manicure. 1800: Blow out the candles. 1801: Party.

The Sergeant was wringing his hands, actually wringing them, first the right, then the left.

"Sergeant?"

"We can't...." He trailed off. Then his eye lit up, inspired. "We don't have any mail bags, ma'am."

"Grab your bed sheets and start sewing. The mail will be sorted and ready to load onto the carrier tomorrow. At o-nine-hundred hours."

"No.... I mean, yes. Yes, ma'am." The Sergeant backed up a few steps, saluted, and bustled—really bustled this time—to the barracks.

The Captain visited the hut with the fly curtain—the sergeant's quarters as it turned out. A jumble of toiletries on the bureau. Fly-specked family pictures. A sweat-stained mattress and a moth-eaten wool blanket of ancient issue.

So what was the good cabin for? They got visitors maybe once in a blue moon. Employee of the month?

A stack of paper, some with corners torn, lay face down on the

Sergeant's bureau, on top of a bandanna. The Captain hesitated. But somehow she doubted the porn would be the mean kind. She flipped the stack over.

Sheer surprise made her laugh.

The Virgin Mary. Buddha. Jesus. Others she didn't know. Robes of red and yellow, black and white and gray. Turbans, loin-cloths, kimonos. Arabic writing. Krishna, Saint Francis, the last Dalai Lama, Black Elk. Drawings, printed cards, clippings from books or magazines.

The bandanna made an island of clean on the scratched, grimy bureau.

The Captain placed the pictures back on it, just so.

When she stepped out of the hut, still smiling, a bunch of men at the barracks doorway murmured. They looked worried or tentatively hopeful. Maybe they'd all added a picture or two, took turns dusting and polishing. The good cabin, her quarters, was their chapel. And she would sleep in there. She resisted the impulse of an apologetic smile, but she did give them a nod. The men grinned and shuffled. Relieved, maybe, that she wasn't going to kick it apart.

She headed to the post office to check on progress or lack thereof. As soon as she stepped inside, the Sergeant pushed the door closed.

The room's quiet distanced the jungle. Hot as an oven, but at least not as humid as outside. One-eye Sergeant sat on the floor with Jaundice Yellow and a one-armed Black soldier.

Unbelievable.

The Captain joined them. She picked up one of the envelopes. Addressed to a private, metered. Civilian business of some kind, not likely to pose a threat to national security, whatever that was. No cause for inspection. But the Captain drew her M3 knife and slit it open.

A nasty piece from a collections agency. The kid should never have been set loose with so much credit, but such was the way of the world. He'd bought more electronics than he could afford, or his wife had a baby, or they'd filled up a state-side apartment with new furniture. Now she sat there, alone, or maybe with a couple of kids, wondering how they would ever pay for it all.

The Captain picked out another envelope, handwritten, addressed to a Major stationed up in the highlands, from a girl or woman with the same last name. She stuck the tip of the M3 under the flap—stopped. She put the envelope down unopened.

Mail was made to carry news, information. Sentiments, if of a personal nature.

Documents from attorneys, from collectors, utilities. Catalogs. News of graduations, promotions. Weddings. Divorce. Failure, fire, flood. Births. Death and love and everything in between.

A captain sent a letter to her son. His reply: a photo of himself, his beautiful skin all marked up, tattooed.

A letter from a man or a woman or a child to a brother, a friend, a sister, a daughter, a father, a son, a mother, a husband, a wife, a lover.

One-arm passed a canteen. Sweat-salt made his dark skin ashy. As the Captain drank, a sense of helplessness took her. It was like when things went wrong with her son or her ex. She usually didn't let it come over her while on duty.

She opened an envelope. A little boy to his sister, a nurse. School, parents, TV shows. Tears for Misty, a cat that died.

The men watched her intently, as if to memorize a new procedure. But she didn't know what she was doing. No. She knew exactly what she was doing. She was breaking the law, perusing other people's mail. What gave her the right? Was she going to check out the whole pile? Her job was to make sure it got sorted and on the carrier, period.

A magazine full of poems. A letter with a bunch of wedding photos enclosed. A solicitation for a lakeside property.

When the window filled with the gaudy hues of sunset, the Captain stood. The Sergeant and One-arm helped Yellow to his feet.

"O-nine-hundred hours," the Captain said. She couldn't tell if they were relieved or disappointed when she said she'd skip dinner.

At the threshold of her quarters—the chapel—she removed her boots. The bed linens were so clean, she thought of looking for a shower, but she just stripped to panties and singlet, and lay down.

Buddha. Jesus. Mary Mother of God. Black Elk. The Dalai Lama. Krishna. St. Francis. Allah's name. Maybe they'd left Earth, too, the holy ones, gone to a better place, leaving behind only their images.

She woke in the night to the racket of reptiles and insects, and herself breathing. She sat up, groped for matches, and lit the candle. Before putting her bare feet on the floor, she looked down to make sure the scorpion hadn't come back. Her sweat and dust imprinted the white sheets. A bottle of Italian mineral water of all things stood by the door, and she opened it and drank. She brought her penlight outside, found a likely place, searched the vicinity for vermin, and squatted. The wet, jungly, dark night jabbered loud, sinister.

Back inside the cabin, the Captain stood in front of the table. She opened its one drawer.

A single picture lay in the middle, a postcard of a god—Hindu, it looked like. He sat cross-legged on a square dais in a garish landscape of flowers, trees, frolicking animals, and a rippling blue lake. Little people carrying pitchers and trays of fruit and other things stood on rainbow-edged clouds. The Captain turned the picture over. Not Hindu. Under a line of exotic script, it said "The Tibetan Deity of Wisdom."

The Captain couldn't help noticing that the god's skin color matched that of the jaundiced soldier. In one hand, he held up a sword. In the other, a flower supporting what looked like a neat stack of envelopes. The Captain smiled, though of course it wasn't mail, but a long, narrow book. She put the picture on the table, propped against the wall, and lay down again.

She dreamt that the water bottle held ink, and she drank it down, and it was bitter and unendingly sweet. She dreamt of opening some books and leaving others closed. She listened to profound discourses.

A timid knock. She sat up blinking. Pale morning. She pulled the sheet up to cover herself.

A female soldier holding a mess tray peered through the screen. She had all four limbs, and her skin glowed with health, and she had both eyes, but they were addled.

"Just put it on the steps there, soldier."

The young woman put the tray down and ran off, the dust puffing clouds under her feet.

The Captain scrubbed a hand through her hair, dressed. She sat on the steps to eat the breakfast, a glop of grits decorated with molasses that looked like motor oil, a hardboiled egg, and burned coffee. A fresh bottle of water. She tried to remember the words in the dream. She wasn't sure they'd been in English, though she'd understood them. The scorpion crept from under the steps and she dropped a piece of egg in the dust, in case scorpions liked such delicacies. Happy birthday. She went to the post office.

The Sergeant, Yellow, and One-arm busily stuffed mail in a mix of mail pouches and nylon laundry bags. Other mail remained stacked behind the door. The Captain wouldn't have been surprised to find there the unopened letter to the Major in the highlands. In their minds, she guessed, the mail was sorted and ready to be loaded on the carrier.

Sooner or later, the mail had to leave here. All of it. Everyone whose name was in the "to" part of the envelopes would have to find out what was written inside.

The chop and whine of a carrier broke her thoughts. She banged out the post office door, took the steps in one leap. The three men straggled after her. She hadn't even heard it, and here it was, practically on their heads, hours early. It lowered over the road, thrashing up towers of dust.

She bolted to her cabin, grabbed her kit, ran back out into the whirling cloud. The Sergeant and Yellow and One-arm gaped up as if one of their gods had come to take them out of here.

"Get that mail!" the Captain yelled over the whomping blades and shrilling engine.

The pilot wouldn't touch down. He hovered above the road as a couple of grinning soldiers dumped bundles of supplies out the bay. The men on the ground heaved the mail bags in. The Captain threw her kit. One of the carrier soldiers almost fell out catching it, his buddy hauling him back by his belt. The carrier's motor wound higher.

The Captain tore her M3 knife from her belt and clapped the hilt into Yellow's hands. She ran under the carrier. The two soldiers were laughing their asses off, but they dropped flat on the deck, reached out of the bay, and managed to take hold of her wrists. As they hauled her up, one thought nailed the Captain's mind: Had the carrier tilted at the wrong moment her hands would have been sliced clean off. Her eyes and mouth filled with dust.

By the time the Captain wept the grit from her eyes and looked out the bay, the depot was gone: the post office, the hut with the fly-curtain, the dirty latrines, the wounded men and their chapel. Below, only jungle.

• • •   • • •

The Tragedy of Gentleman

THE SOUR SCENT of the courier's agitation cut through even the stench of two hundred or so knights eating. With his signal chiming in my earpiece, I rose and wended through the mess hall to the entry, where he waited. The newer knights fell silent as I passed, knowing me for QL's spy. The more seasoned did not bother, knowing that as long as they are loyal, I have nothing to say about them. They did eye me, speculating no doubt how it might affect them, this business that bade me leave QL's table midmeal.

The courier handed over the pod. Unannounced and hand-delivered: the originator dared not risk the message being hacked. Or simply lost to interference. The storm Outside has already knocked out a dozen or so relays. I dismissed the courier and found a secluded nook near the impluvium.

I breached the pod's seal. I listened to the message. I listened to it again. Again.

It is not my place to delay even for a moment passing a message to QL. Yet I delayed. For several moments.

One of QL's secretaries described my reports as "sterile." He even speculated they were framed by a robot. I am not a human, strictly speaking. That does not mean I am a machine. I needed those several moments to gather a semblance of poise.

I requested by direct call a private and immediate audience with QL. She led me not to her quarters, but to a service corridor. She opened a door, looked in, closed it, tried another, and another.

Precautions against surveillance are, for me, habitual. I "record" this diary, for example, only in my thoughts, a private archive. Yet I would not have expected QL to shun her own quarters. Then again, they are no longer her own. Nothing is, in this Domain. It remains mapped as Domain 02, but everyone now calls it Lovely Domain, after QL's eldest daughter.

Does QL distrust Lovely's security? Or does she distrust Lovely herself?

I do.

Finally, a linens closet satisfied. I followed QL in, fighting the ignoble impulse to run away. Or to lie. Or to drop dead. Anything. QL had disowned her youngest daughter, yet the message in my charge would convey to her the deepest woe.

To speak closer to her ear, I climbed atop a hamper. Amidst stacks of tablecloths, towels, and bedsheets reeking of bleach, I recited the message.

GENTLEMAN: Princess was murdered. Hanged or garroted.

QL shut her eyes and took a deep, quick breath. I forced myself to the finish.

GENTLEMAN: The crime was committed in Serene Domain. Perpetrator unknown as of origin time of message.

Having discharged my duty, I waited, steady and quiet, even as sorrow again washed through me. Such cozy times we had as children, Princess and I! Even after rank and maturity distanced us, she always kept a smile for me. And it was she who insisted on my "humanness."

QL gave a brief nod of dismissal.

Aside from that initial gasp, I observed no fault in QL's composure. That is not saying much. She is master of her face, and given she had said not a word, I had no chance to read her voice. Her perfume, which I myself tested, conceals her moods and emotions.

I had barely left the closet when orders came by broadcast: QL will depart for Serene Domain at hour 15.

I could not help noticing, as the knights bustled from the mess hall, the contrast between Lovely's impeccably arrayed troops and ours. The plain truth is, QL's is an army of goons, of ugly, dirty, thuggish men and women. Their war games, not to mention their debauchery, could just about wreck a Domain. Ask our host, Lovely.

Nevertheless, as soldiers they are all discipline. Every transport launched at precisely hour 15. Credit must be shared with Lovely herself. Even amidst her own preparations to depart, she efficiently facilitated the exit of QL's knights, and QL herself, from her newly gotten Domain.

By the way, her body gave off not a whiff of sisterly grief, though her face wore somber decorum.

End of entry.

• • •

2491.05.16.03

OUR JOURNEY GOES less smoothly than our departure. The storm renders navigational instruments all but useless, forcing repeated halts as the pilots seek direction from relay stations. Ozone giants—riled by the constant sheets of lightning, I think, not driven against us—have forced two detours so far. One of the vehicles got mired and nearly engulfed by a slime divil.

I pity the knights in their rough transports. Gloomy as is QL's transport this day, it affords a comfortable and fairly safe journey. A bath chamber allows me to sluice myself often enough to keep my skin from cracking. I believe Princess told QL's steward my needs; I would never presume.

Sweet Princess, may flights of angels sing thee to thy rest!

(Angel: An Old Earth creature, humanlike and winged, whose duty was to protect young humans and, failing that, to lead their dead selves to a palace in outer space whose residents enjoy gentle and unending pleasure.)

This stretch of subdued idleness allows me to catch up with you, dear diary. And to speculate on the identity of the killer. Not that my efforts bear fruit. My talent lies in surveillance, not deduction.

This much I have learned since the message arrived. Yestereve, Princess arrived at Serene in hopes of reconciling with her mother, and to re-open peace negotiations between FR her husband and QL her mother.

No peace bodes now. If FR's spies—I have never succeeded in identifying them, but they are around—managed to break through the storm's interference to convey the dismal tidings of this day, FR surely hurries toward Serene with deadly intent. He loved Princess. Did my loyalties not lie firmly with QL, I would wish him gods' speed.

End of entry.

•••

2491.05.16.12

SERENE DOMAIN'S OFFICIAL guidebook lists the structure in which Princess was laid out as a replica of an Old Earth devotional chapel. Its gray quarry-stone walls and pavement are unadorned, the guidebook claims, to facilitate religious cogitation. To me, the effect is of gloom.

A cold pinlight bathed the robed and veiled figure on the bier at center, leaving all else in shadow. The chilly depths of the vault whispered and echoed with the priests' chants. I stood on a cushioned bench just out of reach of the light, where I could observe all.

QL stood at the head of the bier. Lovely and Regal, QL's eldest and second daughters, respectively, stood with their consorts at the foot. A handful of knights and dignitaries were assembled in the nave.

FR was represented only by those who had traveled to Serene with Princess: a lady's maid and an elderly pilot. Princess had refused to bring her own security. She had said, according to the report of her arrival at Serene: I come in peace to pay reverence to my honored and beloved mother.

And we not here to receive her.

O dismal, dismal hour!

Her soul will disport itself, if the priests' incantations are effective, in the far-away pleasure palace of the youthful dead.

It should be a comfort.

It is not. I want her here, in Serene. Alive, that is.

One spark of happiness glowed within me through the drear proceedings: Fool stood at my side. Our reunion both shamed and gladdened me. Shamed, because I had not possessed the courage to stand with it when QL exiled it from court. (Ever my friend, Fool extolled my timidity as loyalty to QL). Gladdened, because Fool's presence means it again enjoys QL's good graces, and we two can again enjoy each other's company.

All Fool and I have in common is nearly all we have, dear diary, and can be boiled down to one trait: indeterminacy. Gender, station, personhood—all's a blur. Fool wears its confusion frankly, in motley. I go in drab as Gentleman, though no kind of man am I.

We both were plucked from boggy nests, dried, fed, and schooled, our first "people" long-forgotten. (Mutually forgotten, I hope. I would hate for them to come looking for me!) Both smulkins, we, but luck it was that truly bound us: we never got placed in a Works. After some dislocations, we climbed the ranks together, literally from the ground up.

Once upon a time, side by side, cheek by jowl, we handled corpses. Ready to juggle skulls, Fool was, and to banter with mortality, ever the wit, with me as sober-bones sidekick. Graduated (now reinstated) to QL's fool, Fool remains a fellow of infinite jest, easily setting the table on a roar with gibes, gambols, and scrofulous songs.

I, called Gentleman, am a spy, whose dry observations QL has ever heeded. Alas, she rarely heeds Fool's fecund insights. If she did, Princess's husband FR would be no longer our enemy but our valued friend. And Princess would be alive.

The murmuring chants fell silent. The priests withdrew; the corpse handlers waited their turn.

At QL's gesture, an attending knave pinched, as delicately as a man of his ilk could, the bottom two corners of the head veil, and drew them back to reveal the face of our Princess.

A murmuring sigh broke forth from the knights. Though they surely could not see much.

I myself saw too much of what I hoped never to see in this life of mine.

A few discreet stitches held closed poor Princess's choke-bulged eyes. Heavy paint masked the skin. A length of silk bound her jaws, holding in the tongue, likely darkened and swollen, and continued on to wind around her neck, concealing the ligature's marks. Perfume just about soaked the gown; nevertheless, nothing can conceal the rankness of a body violently slain.

QL clasped her daughter's hands.

QL: She's warm!

Only Fool and I, and maybe the knave, could have heard QL's soft cry. She drew in a breath, as if she would call a physician to aid—

The knave dropped the veil, gasped, fumbled it up again…

Too late.

QL's mouth hardened. Her hands remained on her daughter's hands, heavy and gauche. Finally she lifted her hands and nodded. The knave lay down the veil as delicately as he'd lifted it, though paler he was, now. He'd stolen from QL the last moments of her daughter's warmth. He surely knew he deserved to be whipped.

But after all, the young woman dead all these hours, the flesh would have been icy. Only a mother's hope enlivened for a moment those corpsy limbs.

End of entry.

• • •

2491.05.17.14

AFTER THE SERVICE, we adjourned to the e-room. "We" being: QL, QL's minister Naphto, Lovely Consort, Fool, and me. Note who was not present: Lovely herself, Regal and Regal Consort. No surprise, the Regals left out. Lovely, I admit, should probably have been with us.

Lovely Consort beckoned me to a secure monitor.

Lovely Consort: Gentleman, if you please.

I climbed into the seat before the console. Lovely Consort stood close enough for me to catch his scent. Not that it revealed much. Though disdaining the use of perfumes, he always has been a close one. I sensed only some emotional turmoil, by no means excessive: more simmering wrath than grief.

I never could fathom his feelings toward Princess. When she came to nest in QL's womb, QL's lawful consort (now defunct) had been invalided by war wounds. Rumor claimed that it was Lovely Consort (then unmarried, called Yres) who sired Princess, not the maimed man. I believe it. He is virile, well-made, and possesses natural command, and Princess did bear a certain resemblance to him.

Lovely Consort: Gentleman, scan back over the last forty hours.

The span of time since we got news of Princess. The storm brewing fierce by then, the vid rendered mere fragments of light and color—

A span coalesced. I touched pause.

Gentleman (me, that is): This shows drone vid from about two kilometers above central Barren Plain, taken on date 05.16, hour 14.

I touched slo-mo. Though it was the best vid yet, it took a while to analyze. The images flickered, staggered, broke up, froze, unfroze. I back-played a few minutes, touched slo-mo again.

Gentleman (highlighting a section of the display): The moving cluster comprises some 800 countable objects, mostly vehicles. The pattern of their movement indicates an army with a force of approximately 100 squares. Based on FR's previous movements, the arrangement of his troops and the darkish—

Lovely Consort: Yes, yes, to the point.

I paused, not to defy him, but to continue my thoughts inwardly: and the darkish tint of the objects, it is virtually certain that…

GENTLEMAN: It is virtually certain that the cluster is FR's army.

True, no one needed that degree of detail. I never express an opinion or pretend to know what I do not know; hence, it is a given that my summaries are based on data and sound reasoning. I suspect he already knew the situation anyway. The demonstration was made for QL.

LOVELY CONSORT: Forward to date 05.17, hour 9, same coordinates.

The storm by then in full fury, the vid offered only glimpses of the area, but they sufficed.

GENTLEMAN: The cluster is gone.

LOVELY CONSORT: See if you can find him, Gentleman.

I flicked through every viewpoint. The only data I gathered was that ozone giants had knocked the drones all a-hoo.

GENTLEMAN: The drones are disabled. The latest intelligible image is the one we just viewed together.

QL: It's enough. A womb of war, the Barren Plain. FR marches to us.

LOVELY CONSORT: We're fit to meet him.

QL: With justice in his ranks.

FOOL: And our realm all cut in pieces, ho ho.

LOVELY CONSORT: Oh, shut it, Fool.

He made a swatting gesture at Fool, perhaps only in jest, or he might have made a palpable hit, were it not for QL's proscription on physical contact between humans and smulkins. Self-controlled he is, yet Lovely Consort possesses a hasty and violent temper, as many humans do.

FOOL: Poor Fool, o me o my.

> It smirked, but its scent revealed to me deep unhappiness. Minister Naphto cleared his throat.

NAPHTO: We will send our army Outside, will we not? A siege is a dismal thing, after all.

> His words, thought I, were surely impassioned by the likelihood that FR's initial assault would be made on Naphta subDomain, to cripple manufacturing and to stage from there an attack or siege on the main of Serene Domain.

FOOL: We have not an army, dear Minister. We have three! Imagine! Three armies!

> No one acknowledged the jest, or its meaning: that Lovely's and Regal's prematurely granted inheritance had sliced QL's force into three.

LOVELY CONSORT: Yes. If we must war, let the battlefield be ours to choose.

FOOL: Zing diddy ho ho.

> A nice punctuation to Lovely Consort's agreement with Naphto, different as were their arguments.

QL: Go, then, Lovely my son, and meet our enemy. While you destroy him, we will stay here to make common cause with him.

A brief bow, and off he went, no questions asked, his steps brisk and light, musclebound though he is, and no longer young.

He will easily be gone by next day's end, for he keeps himself and his troops ever honed to make war. No love for hearth and home anchors him. He dislikes domesticity, and he detests his wife, their marriage a veritable encyclopedia of discord. He detests, too, his wife's rank. When Lovely came into her Domain, her rise lifted him to First Rank—but only as her consort.

And who would not gladly escape the coils of the palace intrigue that killed Princess? Yes, dear diary, it may seem that the Princess was killed by patriots, to keep Serene Domain from her consort FR's reach. To Fool and me, at least, it's plain that Princess was killed to put Serene in reach of Lovely and Regal. It is a Domain to covet.

Counting its subDomains (including Naphto's property), Serene is enormous. Nearly 8,000 acres! The quality of its plexi and the subtly changing lumens of its oculi give the Domain, they say, an Old Earth feel. Indeed, its sobriquet Serene is, according to the guidebook, after an Old Earth city that united perfectly water, stone, fire, and sky, until, so the story goes, even its marble palaces gave way to the rain. (Marble: A hard yet corruptible Old Earth composite of minerals quarried for statuary, monuments, and buildings.)

Fool puns that Serene is a-mazing. True. Its dwellings and enterprises lie not on a graceless grid, like those of Lovely Domain. Rather, they follow a mazelike spiral of walkways, courtyards, and canals.

Canals? Yes! Flaunting its superiority to all other domains, Serene strives not to keep water out. It lets water in, to form graceful, winding channels. Watercraft ply our streets, their pace leisurely and quiet. Many a night, with only the starry domes to wink down on us, Fool and I have raced through Serene, stretching our half-atrophied gills to their utmost, contesting who will find the shortest and quickest way to this campo, that palace. Even Naphta subDomain boasts a certain gritty charm (though nothing would induce me to swim its polluted waters).

In days of yore I prayed that, though youngest of QL's daughters, Princess would come to hold Serene. She was her mother's favorite, right up to the disastrous moment QL denounced her. Never did I give up hope that QL would love her again.

Now Serene Domain will stay caught in the teeth of Lovely and Regal. QL's "gift" of it to them comprises merely a few ambiguous and impulsive words—words uttered by QL herself, unfortunately, in the presence of several high-ranking witnesses.

One great, ameliorating factor remains on our side: Minister Naphto's subDomain adjoins Serene. This proximity, together with Lovely's and Regal's long-borne animus toward Naphto, spurs him to toil day and night to keep Serene in QL's possession. Naphto may not be much of a man, but he does have a gift for manipulating law. I pray he succeeds.

Or maybe I should not pray. My prayers go awry, and I am very attached to Serene.

Lovely Consort's jaunty step had barely faded, when Naphto burst forth with every persuasion to the end that QL rescind her bellicose orders and go forth to embrace FR. How rash we are, he argued, to destroy any chance of peace—a peace for which Princess gave her life!

Fool and I listened in agreement no less fervent for being silent. And confused. Had Naphto not just advised we send out an army? His new counsel did not merely revise his previous; it turned from it 180 degrees.

180 degrees—or pick any number—his change of mind mattered not. QL's purpose was fixed. She would have FR punished for having allowed Princess to meet her death.

Naphto's next argument took yet another turn.

NAPHTO: Madam, should you not then join your prowess to that of Lovely Consort in the field of valor?

QL: Nay. Here we will work to appease our enemy, my daughter's consort, over her dead body. We will find and inch to a miserable death those responsible for the foul deed that did her in.

> A mother's wrath, not even Fool dared mock.
> Naphto looked positively sunk.
> Aha.
> *End of entry.*

• • •

2491.05.17.18

DESPITE HIS INGRAINED paranoia, Naphto is easier to surveil than most other humans. He is remarkably unaware of his physical surroundings. Rarely have I had to camo myself to avoid his detection. This time was no exception.

As I slipped along after him—not to his own quarters but rather, as I had expected, to Embarcadero NE—I reviewed his zigzag arguments at the conference. What they boil down to is this: he wants QL and her men gone, gone, and gone from Serene Domain. He fears QL herself more than a foreign invasion, for despite her baffling perfume, and even before she adjourned our meeting with her dire sentence, the stench of her wrath was surely clear even to human senses.

Personal culpability was not what cowed him. He had no reason to employ an assassin to kill Princess. He cherished no deadly grudge against her, and he had supported the peace negotiations for which she unwittingly sacrificed herself. Besides, he is just not the type. Rather, he held a suspicion, perhaps a certainty, that someone close to him is guilty.

It was easy to guess who that someone might be.

At the Embarcadero, he boarded a private gondola. A little tricky, to get myself on board unobserved, but I managed. No way would I burn my eyes raw, swimming into Naphta subDomain, his obvious destination. It would not have helped to camo myself, either, the visual environment being too irregular.

He (we) disembarked at Crystal, a bauble of a sector where high-ranking folk tuck their cast-off paramours and less-than-illustrious offspring, and where every form of debauchery is for sale. There, in a shabby mansion, dwells his older son B-one.

Some family history will illuminate the coming "scene."

Naphto has two children, both male. The younger, A-two, sprang from Naphto's lawful wife, a highborn woman who died birthing him. The elder, B-one, is a by-blow whose making his father publicly boasts as "good sport." Were it lousy sport, or indifferent, I suppose B-one's fate would be as obscure as that of his mother. Who knows what outlet his tendencies would have found? Peddling drugs and human flesh, I imagine. In return for the memorable pleasure of his making, Naphto granted B-one the mansion in Naphta subDomain (though he himself would not dream of living there), a generous allowance, and no expectation of more.

B-one: Whoreson. A-two: True. It is how I sort them out.

Before following Naphto into the mansion, I paused to slip off my gown and tuck it into my tummy pouch (as Princess used to call the envelope of skin on my abdomen), and camo'd myself. B-one's powers of observation far surpass those of his father.

A niche near the central stairway afforded me discreet aural and olfactory access to the meeting of father and by-blow son. The last time I surveilled B-one, I shared that niche with a statue of a male athlete. Sold off, like the rugs, chandeliers, furniture, and whatever else B-one could pry loose to fund his recreational habits. Only the pedestal remained. It sufficed. I crouched behind it and uncamo'd my skin. The curious pattern of the mansion's walls made camo more tiring even than usual to sustain. Unfortunately, I left my gown tucked away, planning to re-camo before leaving the hiding place.

Father and son greeted each other with every show of affection, but Naphto's voice revealed his tension.

NAPHTO: What is it you were reading when I came in?

B-ONE: Nothing much.

B-one's perfume is merely ornamental, but his voice is well-baffled. Some even believe it is a machine lodged in his throat. Not so. A drug inhalation habit has made him a basso profundo without the usual degree of resonance.

A *plumph* as Naphto (he is fat) settles on a cushioned chair.

NAPHTO: Let's see it.

B-ONE: Really, father, it's nothing.

NAPHTO: Come, come.

During the long silence that followed, presumably Naphto reading the paper, I crept from the niche to test the air more thoroughly.

A whiff of Lovely, a few days old. No surprise there. Her consort often and gratefully absent, she has been conducting a liaison with B-one for some time. Not a whisper of gossip has it raised. I may be the only one who knows, outside the two of them and QL herself. Not so, the affair between—among?—B-one and Regal and Regal Consort.

B-one may find "good sport," to use his father's phrase, in

playing these sex games (especially with Regal and Regal Consort, given their common proclivities), but he has not the slightest affection for his fellow players. He is in it for himself. None of the players, in fact, possess hearts to be broken.

QL took no action, following my report of it. Harmless, the goings on, seemed to be the verdict. Now I think, maybe not so harmless. B-one himself is by no means harmless. Among the more quotidian smells—human, perfume, fun-chem—a bouquet of other scents haunts his quarters. In particular, smulkin. He professes a sympathy for "our planet's peoples," but plainly his interest derives not from concern for the well-being of native fauna or what have you. He may be a "natural" son, but he is neither a natural person, nor a naturalist. He wants to agitate labor to discomfit his father. But when a human uses smulkins to make trouble, it is the smulkins who get the trouble.

Naphto suddenly emitted a sharp odor, a signal of distress so tangible I could nearly taste it. Yet no actual danger was manifest!

B-ONE: Dad, it's nothing.

NAPHTO: The two of you, together?

B-ONE: Never.

NAPHTO: Just him, then.

A slight hesitation.

B-ONE: It's not what it seems.

Another hesitation.

B-ONE: He's … dissembling. A joke.

However altered the voice, the arhythms of human speech

cannot be baffled. The timing of B-one's hesitations revealed not honest doubt but a deliberate casting of doubt.

A silence; probably Naphto again perused the paper.

His distress would have seemed to answer affirmatively the question of whether B-one could be incriminated in Princess's murder, but I suspected some other game afoot. Although Naphto had dropped in unannounced, to catch B-one unaware, clearly B-one had staged the scene of his father's arrival: letter in hand and, perhaps, a startled gesture to raise Naphto's suspicions and to provoke the demand to examine the paper.

I wondered how B-one learned Naphto was coming. No surveillance, electronic or organic, operates in his mansion, or on his or Naphto's person. Was there an informer en route—the ferryman or a security guard? Or maybe he simply looked out a window. I congratulated myself on entering the mansion in camo.

B-ONE: Come, father. It's nothing, I swear.

A crinkle of paper, a tap, a skittering: presumably B-one took back the paper, wadded it up and tossed it onto some surface, probably the floor, where it bounced-slid several centimeters.

B-ONE: Only a jest.

NAPHTO: A very ugly jest.

B-ONE: Agreed. I'll speak with him.

NAPHTO: Needless to say…

Inwardly, I finished the sentence: say nothing to QL.

B-ONE: Of course.

NAPHTO: You are satisfied with your portion, are you not?

B-ONE: Satisfied and grateful, father.

Suddenly, unexpectedly—without parting words, Naphto exited the chamber. Worse, on stepping into the hall, he turned in the wrong direction.

I had not the time to hide or camo myself.

He froze, eyes wide, mouth gaping. Then, with a little scream, he scurried off.

I ducked back behind the pedestal, hoping that B-one would not come out to see what was going on. To my relief, he did not.

I do not think my presence in itself startled Naphto so badly. He expects me to sneak around after him and anyone else I find appropriate to surveil. It was me, myself, that made him … squeak.

I go about always in the hooded gown mandated by QL for me and the handful of other non-labor smulkins. Yet I do not perceive myself without it as "naked." Nor has it ever occurred to me that most humans, including Naphto, have no idea what a smulkin looks like unrobed.

Not so odd, I do not think. We are quite humanlike in form, with head and body and two arms and two legs. The external differences are minor. Unless camo'd, our skin is a hairless, pale bluish-gray. The sense organs of the head are more pronounced and numerous. Our "privates" are naturally concealed. We lack weaponlike attributes such as claws, fangs, stingers, and so on. We are small and feeble, relative to adult humans. In a nutshell, we are not scary! Still, Naphto is a timid man, and evidently what merely looks strange is enough to jolt him.

Had that irrational burst of panic not sent him scuttling away, he surely would have tried to negotiate the way in which I will report this visit to QL. Without success. I answer to QL, period. I am hers alone.

On that note, I decided to linger in the niche until B-one left to his evening's pleasures. I could then slip into his chambers to purloin the paper and take a look around. While I waited, I reviewed the meeting between him and his father.

Was B-one satisfied with his portion? Naphto asked. B-one's answer: *Satisfied and grateful.* Two lies in one short utterance.

But we knew that already.

Naphto: The two of you, together.

He meant his two sons, none other, for that is how he sees them, as two always "together." He boasts, even, that the similarity of their appearance makes them twinlike. For all his skills in law and finance, he is a short-sighted man, less able even than most humans to discern currents of emotion. He is soft and thick.

B-one told one truth today: *Never*—the two of them together. In blood, half-brothers; in spirit, unrelated. Much like Princess and her two elder sisters, come to think of it.

A-two's expeditions Outside are, in my view, grotesque. After one glimpse of his trophy room, I keep well away from him. Yet none would say he is not upright. Moreover, dwelling as he does secure in his father's favor, wealth, and future rank, he has nothing to gain or lose from B-one. Brotherly love rests cold but easy in A-two True's heart.

For B-one Whoreson, brotherhood means vain struggle, an allowance that fluctuates at his father's whim, and eternally inferior rank. Whatever the personal advantage—no small consideration to him—he would never enter into any kind of scheme with A-two. His smiles and kisses at family affairs are only for show.

The paper that B-one led Naphto to read also led Naphto to believe that A-two is trying to lure B-one into: *A very ugly jest.* Not an insult, this "jest." Fear dominated Naphto's scent, with wrath and sentimental injury secondary notes. That paper represented, to Naphto, a definite threat.

Summary: B-one contrived to make Naphto suspect that A-two solicited B-one to help kill or damage him. On gaining

Naphto's rank and property A-two would, presumably, reward B-one generously.

If Naphto were not so paranoid, he would see the rats that lurk behind the hangings of the purported plot. (Rat: a foul, devouring, and disease-spreading Old Earth animal that unfortunately thrives in Serene, along with the noble horses and dogs.)

First: A-two already has unlimited access to his father's wealth.

Second: Naphto is old.

Ergo, A-two need not speed his inheritance. He may not be eager for it at all, given the time he spends with his "collections" and his aromachology—at which he is quite gifted, by the way. It was he who blended QL's perfume.

B-one, on the other hand, has every reason for urgency. Once Naphto dies, or if A-two secures Naphto's rank and assets in some other manner, B-one's chance is lost. He must push on, if he will subvert the lack of legacy that is his birthright. The bastard brother cannot afford patience. The game is to get A-two disowned before he owns all, including, basically, B-one himself. B-one's protestations of A-two's innocence served not to defend his brother but to build his own facade of naive, fraternal devotion.

For now, Naphto is happy to believe the letter is a misunderstanding. But doubt will out, a diligent worm nibbling away his peace of mind. (Believe you me, as a former corpse handler, I know what a diligent worm can do!)

How can B-one believe that QL will ever countenance such a ploy? He may be hopelessly debauched, but he is no idiot. Maybe he thinks that QL breaking up the realm in favor of Lovely and Regal means she is "slipping."

Certain sounds and smells indicated that he was settling in to enjoy his evening's pleasures at the domestic hearth. I began to ease out of the niche—

B-ONE: Little Gentleman, come in here.

I considered taking my chances with the nearest canal and swimming off. But flight would have served nothing at all. It certainly would not serve QL, I thought.

Belatedly, I donned my gown and went in there.

Never before had I been in B-one's inner sanctum, but it held no surprises. Like the rest of his mansion, it was sparsely furnished, the most elaborate object being a multi-user bong. The sole light filtered through a window with colored panes. The dimness was pleasant—most humans require very bright illumination—but the smells in the stuffy room were distasteful, as was his familiarity. He gestured me to sit not on the couch, but with him, on the floor. I took one of the under-stuffed cushions and politely refused his offer of refreshment.

I thought I knew what he wanted. He would entwine his own conspiracy with the plight of labor, assuming that as a smulkin I would happily sign on to the cause.

Wrong.

B-ONE: Do you know, little Gentleman, that I was a member of the expedition that captured you?

I did not answer, and not only because the question took me by surprise. I doubted he expected an answer, any more than I had expected his question. Truth: I did not know anything about said expedition, being but an infant at the time.

B-ONE: My brother invited me. Yes, the man whose relationship with our mutual father I'm working hard to destroy.

I said nothing. I did note, though, that his perfume had not been blended by A-one. I traced it to an aromachologist not far from the Molo. Not only did it do nothing to conceal his scent; in some odd way, it seemed to enhance elements of it.

B-ONE: He has a great interest in monsters, as he calls them.

So do I call them monsters.

B-ONE: Gobbledeens, ozone giants—or rather, traces of ozone giants. Swamp roaches. Slime divils. If he can't capture them alive, he kills them on the spot. He then brings them to his laboratory and preserves them. He has a room full of what he calls specimens.

True.

B-ONE: I always refused his safari invitations. The whole thing sickened me.

He smiled the way humans do to announce irony.

B-ONE: Not that I'm a vegetarian or anything soft-hearted like that. The gods only know why I accepted, that time. Well, I do know why. I still suffered the illusion that getting in good with my brother would get me in good with my father. Put the man's two sons on equal footing. And could it be that I cherished a hope for something like true brotherly love? Who knows? This World of ours does hold some strange mutations, for which we must angle in a lake of darkness.

I suppose he meant, humans act on motives obscure even to themselves.

B-ONE: So. I went. A-two brought along, as is his custom, a security detail and plenty of weapons. And cages. And restraints. And so on.

None of this was new to me. I have accompanied QL on similar expeditions, though with purposes practical, not scientific: when a relay station suffered an outage from ozone giants, when a slime divil took up lodgings in one of Serene's water feeds. Most recently, when gobbledeens invaded Lovely Domain.

You know, the cursed campaign that took us away from Serene while Princess journeyed here.

B-one's account held no interest, but duty bade me stay.

B-ONE: Less than a day Outside, a gang of gobbledeens trashed one of our vehicles. I was amused. My brother was not. He expressed the belief that, were they not —

He clawed the air with two fingers of each hand. A quotation, forthcoming.

B-ONE: —contained (claw, claw), they would multiply and attack the domes. My belief is that being outwitted infuriated him. Got his blood up. When a group of smulkins raided our supplies the next morning and made off with a bale of food, he and a dozen or so men went hot in pursuit. They returned to camp covered with— with blood. If that is the correct term.

Most humans are unable to "read" smulkins, but given his association with labor, I could not count on that. I kept my face carefully nondescript. But he was not looking at me. He stared at the bong.

B-ONE: It does not run red.

Correct. It is purple.

B-ONE: On our way back to the dome, we found you. Where I saw an untidy but snug den in which dwelt twelve plump baby smulkins clambering for their dinner, my brother saw ... squalor. He claimed you'd been abandoned, that smulkins have no affection for their children.

That I knew, pretty much. I mean, I knew we'd been abandoned.

Assumed to be abandoned, to be exact. Princess once cuddled me, weeping: *How could anyone aba*ndon you?

B-ONE: So we—(again, the air clawing) —rescued you. All of you.

That is how Princess put it, without the facetious quotations around the word "rescued."

B-one unhooked a mouthpiece from the bong, clicked, inhaled.

B-ONE (voice pinched from holding in the vapor): Three survived the journey here. Of those, two soon died in a Works. (Gusting exhale.) You, the poor Princess kept.

I got up, bowed politely.

GENTLEMAN: Thanks be.

He could take that however he liked.

Upon my return to QL's domicile, I reported the entire episode, from Naphto's meeting with B-one, to B-one's account of his brother's safari.

QL did not… She did not respond.

Not that she did, normally. But she did not seem to attend to a word I said.

End of entry.

• • •

2491.05.18.14

WITH ENTIRE MANSIONS at her disposal on her succession, QL chose a domicile relatively modest in dimension, but gracious and airy, and full of shimmering light. Serene's most sought-after decorator created of it a refuge of comfort and elegance.

Or so it used to be. QL's clothes, armor, jewels and so forth still occupy closets and chests. But the climate controls were left off in her absence and all is dank, even musty. Some choice furniture and artworks have been removed; the couch on which QL sits brooding looks to have been appropriated from an inferior lounge. (Fool's and my belongings still crowd the room we share, no one having bothered to pilfer our dowdy gowns and paltry trinkets.) Dust lies thick wherever a cursory swipe would not reach. The goldfish pool is scum-rimmed, its little jungle of potted plants dead or dying.

The place now figures more as a warren of forgotten storerooms than quarters befitting the woman who seized Serene and battled to keep it and all its riches for her daughters.

What dismays me most is that QL, usually exacting to receive her due—no more, but no less—seems hardly to notice.

Fool and I mulled this over (silently, in a language of gestures all our own), sitting on a few stale floor cushions amongst the potted plants beside the fish pool.

GENTLEMAN (in gesture-language): My report on Naphto and B-one raised not even an eyebrow.

In answer, Fool pointed to a poor fish, bobbing dead against the scummy edge of the pool.

GENTLEMAN (in gesture-language): Of course. She is in deep mourning.

A quirk of Fool's mouth said, that was not what it meant; sorrow's gray cast alone could not so dim QL's majesty.

FOOL (in gesture-language): Things have been deteriorating for a while.

Reluctantly, I had to agree. Not long after QL parceled out her realm, Lovely offered to take charge of the staff maintaining QL's domicile here in Serene. QL, having little interest in household affairs as long as they go smoothly, made no objection. At the time, the proposal seemed eminently sensible. Looking back, Lovely's intention becomes clear: she would chip away QL's influence.

As if in answer to our thoughts, Lovely strode into the room. As usual, she ignored us. Or she might not even have noticed us, half-hidden as we were, gratefully, amongst the wilting plants.

GENTLEMAN (in gesture-language): Is there any hope she'll order her staff to get this place in shape?

FOOL (in gesture-language): Ha!

QL greeted her eldest graciously, even lovingly, despite Lovely's glowering countenance.

QL: That frown becomes thee, on this sad day.

Fool broke our cover. Of course.

FOOL: How lovely was Lovely's mother when she cared not for a Lovely frown. Oops! (Grabbing its tongue within its mouth.) The Lovely face bids silence, while Mom stays mum.

QL (to Lovely): Come sit with us.

Lovely plopped onto the couch, but clearly she visited neither to comfort mother nor to mourn sister.

QL: Your consort soon departs to fight the man who sent your little sister into the wilderness.

LOVELY: While my husband chases your whim, your knights will more than ever run riot!

QL (with a slight smile): My knights? Naughty?

Lovely launched a list of the dire offenses. A flagon of ale tipped over a clerk's head at table, some bawdy song in the palace square, a cask of fun-chem illicitly tapped, a beef slaughtered in a mock joust, piss running down a wall, the bowling green gouged up, an overturned gondola.

Oh, dear.

Fool and I could only stifle our laughter.

Hey, it's an army!

And while being an army, they defended the Domains so dearly coveted by this same whining daughter. They breathed in the barbecue that ozone giants made of their comrades. Their bodies gave feast to gobbledeens. They saw their comrades rotted alive, choked by vines, devoured by hasty swamp roaches, suffocated in slime excretions, self-murdered running mad into the everlasting rain. On a personal note: unlike certain favored children of this Domain, our knights keep faithfully QL's order not to molest smulkins. For all their "riot."

Most to the point, Serene is not Lovely's Domain, nor Regal's, hard at it though they grasp. The "deed" of it to them, whether witnessed by one or one thousand humans, remains unratified.

Our self-contained merriment dispersed as quickly as the storm gathered on QL's face. I only hoped she would, for a change, humor Naphto. He had advised QL to avoid any quarrel with Lovely and Regal, given the precarious legal situation of Serene. I also hoped that Fool would hold its tongue—in the figurative sense! He has a knack for breaking Lovely's reserve into laughter, but clearly not on this occasion.

Lovely: We cannot endure the constant brawling, the drunken orgies—which you egg on. Once upon a time, you kept stricter discipline. It's slipping now. You have not been yourself of late.

The traitorous words shamed me, being nearly one with my own recent thoughts.

QL: Not myself? (Looking around.) Can anyone tell me who else I might be?

I gave Fool a precautionary gesture, which it, as usual, ignored.

FOOL: You are your shadow, madam. Or, perhaps, a biddable mother.

QL (to Lovely): And who might you be, woman? Are you my daughter, come to bid me how to boss my men?

Lovely's face hardened. Her mother's ominous calm daunted her not in the least. She is as steely as QL, though without QL's… Whatever it is that makes some humans appealing: warmth, embodiment, authenticity, gallantry.

LOVELY: They conduct themselves as if our Domains were warrens of gobbledeens to be sacked. Rein them in, for the gods' sakes. Better yet, trim them down to those that frame becomingly your dignity and age. Retain your honor guard. Your best men! Let go the rest of the blackguards.

Oh, why could QL not have brushed her off? Say something like, I'll look into it, daughter. And, yes, rein in her knights. Instead, she sprang to her feet and exploded.

QL: Roach-faced bitch! Every man and woman of mine possesses more excellence in one of their battle-grimed fingernails than you possess in your flabby, silk-clad self.

LOVELY (also on her feet): They're out of control! They molest my staff and corrupt my knights. And you unwilling or unable to….

She trailed off as her Consort entered, bulky in full battle dress. I doubt he came to seek a loving cup from his less than beloved wife. Maybe he sought QL's parting blessing. Whatever he wanted mattered not. QL ignored him, furious set as she was on Lovely, saliva literally foaming and flying from her mouth.

QL: They will stay by me, every last one of them! And if I tell them they may run riot in this, my own domain, why then they will turn these domes inside out!

Abruptly, she turned to Lovely Consort.

QL: What business have you here, cock-shriveled wife-son?

Lovely Consort flushed but kept his composure. Or maybe he was already flushed. His armored suit did bundle him up.

Lovely Consort: May I know, madam, what moves you to this wrath?

His glance at Lovely spoke not of commiseration, but blame. Given that he is an ambitious, clever, and political man, he had surely passed to her much the same advice Naphto had passed to QL: Do not pick any fights with your family until Serene is secured.

QL: Sure, sure, son. Sure you know not what this bitch hath blathered. But it joins you as well, so hear my wish.

She drew herself up so rigidly, she trembled.

QL: May your Lovely wife's womb dry up. May it forbid that she ever have children to honor and love her. No. No, on second thought: let her bear! Let her bear children in her exact image! May they thwart and fret her, each moment from each one's birth. May they stamp her face haggard with care and woe, may they gouge wrinkles to hollow out her cheeks and make canals for abundant tears. May her offspring break her heart, then hold her ever after in contempt. As she ages, let them mock her body and mind. May she be pierced deep by the adder's fang that is an ungrateful child!

(Adder: a wormlike Old Earth creature whose bite injects deadly poison into its victim.)

LOVELY CONSORT: By the gods, madam, where does this come from?

Lovely's mouth thinned into a tight smile. I admit, I did feel QL had assailed her harshly. Even Fool looked shaken.

LOVELY: Let her rant. She can't help —

Lovely Consort gripped her arm, hard, judging by her wince and futile attempt to shake him off. He bowed to QL.

LOVELY CONSORT: Madam, my respects.

QL sat heavily on the sofa. She then spoke on, scowling blankly toward the smudged, streaked balcony doors, seeming not to notice that Lovely Consort had bowed his farewell and was half-dragging Lovely with him from the chamber.

QL: When your little sister hears of this, she'll flay with her own fingernails your monstrous face.

Little sister. I wondered, did she mean Princess? QL surely knows that however much Regal hates Lovely, she is hardly apt to fly in her face to defend their mother's honor.

QL (in a muttering growl): And you'll find I'm not so far in dotage as you please. You'll see. You'll see, foul bitch not worthy of the title 'daughter.'

She subsided finally with a groaning sigh. She might have wept a little, I am not sure, for I had directed my attention to Lovely's and her consort's hushed, angry conference in the passage. QL evidently heard nothing of it. Every word, though, carried clearly to me and Fool.

Lovely Consort: What under rain was that all about?

A friction of cloth: Lovely pulling herself loose from her husband. Then strokes as she smoothed her sleeve.

Lovely: I tell you, she's senile.

She gave a little tsk of disdain. Or it could have been a sniff.

Lovely Consort: My wife, you go too far.

Lovely: She wants a plump entourage to cushion her insane impulses, her rash tempers. She enjoys terrorizing us. (Very quietly:) She always has.

I do not say, the last had a ring of truth. But it did ring sincere. I mean, by Lovely's lights, QL has always enjoyed terrorizing her … and Regal, I suppose. Not Princess.

Lovely Consort: Just words.

Lovely: Just words? With just words, she has you happily running off on a futile mission. Then, while you wander Outside, her knights will throw us over. You'll return to nothing, from this abortion of a campaign, with nothing accomplished.

Lovely Consort: You over-fear.

Lovely: Better over-fear than over-trust.

Lovely Consort's only answer was a creak of his armor; maybe he adjusted something.

Lovely: Go fight the old bat's battles. I and those who stand by me will remain here to fight ours.

He did leave, as he no doubt wished all along, his protestations made only in show. I did envy him, in that moment. His manly form so easily cast off domestic coils!

The afternoon trickled by in silence thick and gray as the dust under the furnishings. Fool and I amused ourselves, in our little hideaway among the plants, playing cards with a deck looted from one of FR's minor domains. The knight who gave it to us told that its court cards depicted Old Earth queens, kings, and knaves. The pips bore sigils, arranged in patterns, of tools, weapons, jewels, and human internal organs.

If either of us made to fetch servants, QL called us back. Fool made a stab at putting the food-encrusted lunch dishes outside; QL barked him down. A gesture to light the heater, to open the window covers, even just to tidy up a bit, she made us abandon. She wanted us to be there; she wanted stillness and quiet. We might as well have been the painted figures on the card-board that seemed to moulder even as we played.

After several idle hands, I realized (and so did Fool; our eyes met), she not only brooded. She waited. For Lovely to have a change of heart? For some proper servants to attend us, as they should, without a summons? For news of her new war. For the names of those who killed Princess—an investigation she showed little sign of pursuing. For the evening meal. For a courier to come in with some document requiring her, and only her, attention.

For Princess, whose limbs the corpse handlers would by now have hacked off, to walk through the door.

For things to go back to the way they were.

I smell every drop and morsel QL ingests. I breathe the air she breathes in and the air she breathes out. She is not being poisoned.

End of entry.

● ● ●

2491.05.18.21

THE OCULUS WAS dimming toward night when QL rose with an air of calm resolve.

QL: Come, let's go for a ride.

Our gondola—driven by QL herself; she often enjoys going about without a pilot—soon entered the Grand Canal. Fool and I figured her destination was Regal's palace, an overstuffed and ostentatious structure got by her husband's sharp dealings.

Regal is so addled, it is hard to bear her company. I do not mean "deficient" or "retarded." I mean that steady indulgence in fun-chem renders her unable to follow a line of thought to any purpose. For all that, Fool and I, communicating in gestures, shared our hope that the quiet interval had mellowed QL, and that she was ready to use Regal as a go-between to reconcile with Lovely. It would not be the first time mother and daughter patched up a quarrel like so.

As we passed Palace Square, Fool and I shared a sudden, more urgent hope: that QL would whiz by without seeing what was there. Our prayer was nearly answered when an errant wave, a cursed little wave, changed the peaceful course the evening had taken. The gondola turned slightly. QL glanced over the Square.

The pillory bound one of her knights.

She veered into a parking bay, cut the motor and leapt from the craft with the agility of a young girl.

The knight was clearly shit-faced, listing in his bonds. Nevertheless, public punishment of a man of hers, and without her consent, was outrageous. Beyond outrageous. Treasonous.

We had barely disembarked when Regal and her Consort emerged from the arcade, both reeking of fun-chem.

Regal is muddle-witted, but her Consort is something else altogether. He is gravely damaged, inwardly. Beneath expensive perfumes, he smells rotten. His face is so slackened by debauchery, it appears smudged, indistinct. For all that, his eyes gleam sharp; his wits, unlike his wife's, somehow remain intact. His wife's sister Lovely foamed about rapes and disorder. If rapes and disorders were tallied in these domes, Regal Consort would surely score more than all the knights together.

Regal Servant trailed the couple, its head visibly throbbing at the side, and one leg dragging. I never have liked this one, but always I have pitied it. Fellow feeling, I suppose. Not many of us smulkins live this side of the Works.

To no one's surprise, QL offered no affectionate greeting.

QL: How comes it my knight is pilloried? Who put him there? Regal, I hope this is not by your leave.

Lovely emerged from the arcade, a clear ice in her hand.

QL (turning to her): You. Are you not ashamed to look on me?

LOVELY: Not at all.

Smiling, she clasped Regal's hand. Only hatred for their mother deeper than their mutual antipathy allowed such a spectacle.

QL (to Regal): You let her take your hand?

LOVELY: Why not? We're sisters! Or has age robbed your fond memory of—

QL (to Regal Consort): You, flat-face. How came my man to be pilloried?

REGAL CONSORT (puffing himself up): I put him there, madam.

QL: Did you now? Did you?

REGAL CONSORT: Your knave did abuse and abase my own servant, so we took him in hand. In echo of your own decree, madam.

The drugs that glazed his eyes bolstered his lying bravado. Lying, yes. QL's knight certainly did not inflict those injuries on Regal Servant. The Regals, however, are known to be heavy-handed with their household staff.

QL: You dared?

REGAL: He did dare, and I am with him.

QL: You would not commit this defiance, by the gods.

REGAL CONSORT: We would, by any god you name, pillory any man who would beat our flob.

(Flob: A crass term for smulkin.)

Regal tried to add something, but a giggling fit gibbered her words. I think it was a correction to what her husband said, something along the line of: they would pillory anyone who beat their flob without their leave.

LOVELY: Your knight would not be pilloried had he enjoyed better oversight.

QL: How will I be here?

REGAL (huffing and twitching from her fit of hilarity): You should not be here, Mother. Please. Be sensible. Return to Lovely Domain. We agreed. (To Lovely:) Didn't we? A month at Lovely, while I fix up my domain..... (Giggling.) Well, I guess that won't happen.

A canny guess, given that FR had demolished Domain 03 shortly after Regal got it.

QL turned away. Fool, blessedly silent, and I trailed her toward the gondola. It looked as if the altercation had reached its end, and none too soon.

FOOL (in gesture language): Look on the bright side. As long as they fight, QL lives.

It needed not spelling out: as long as litigation ties up Serene, none can inherit it.

We were just about to board the gondola when QL turned and stalked back to her daughters who themselves were heading back to the arcade. She grabbed Regal's arm and spun her around. Regal did cringe with fear and who could blame her. I feared, myself, that Regal Consort would physically intervene; he has fortitude. Fortunately QL released her hold.

QL: You suggest I stay a term with the slime divil you call sister? She who would diminish my retinue? She who calls my best men blackguards? She who would dispel my force? This was not in our trumped up agreement.

None reminded her, though I could nearly see it hopping off the tip of Regal Consort's tongue, that the "trumped up agreement" had been forged in her own mouth.

QL (to Regal and Lovely): You are not my daughters. I have no daughter.

FOOL: That's true, for you made your daughters your mother, and gave them a whip and lifted your ass over your head for it to be used.

In vain, I gesticulated at it.

FOOL: Oh, how happy for them, and how sad for the ones who love you, that such a ruler as you were should become a fool like me.

REGAL CONSORT: This creature should be whipped. And pilloried.

FOOL: An I lied, would I be spared, mother dear?

GENTLEMAN: Hush, Fool.

Never before had I directed my friend aloud. The force of surprise subdued it. Or Fool took in, at last, that this scene had nothing in it to mock.

LOVELY (to QL): Madam, let you go to Lovely Domain, with your honor guard, and stay for the term agreed upon.

Presumably, with a retinue reduced—to about fifty, I think—and more disciplined, QL would not need Lovely's supervision, and Lovely herself could remain here in Serene, visiting her lover and gaining followers.

QL (quietly): To think I've wrangled with these creatures, these past hours of my precious life. Better parley with a slime divil or a gobbledeen. Better kneel to FR, beg of him a pension. Better I serve your battered flob.

LOVELY: It's your choice, mother.

QL: Then forever shall I keep Serene as my abode.

REGAL CONSORT: With your knights? Lovely's right. These multiple commands, yours and ours, cannot abide under one roof. Tumult, riot, new reaches of debauchery.

QL (laughing, though without humor): You would fear new reaches of debauchery? Come now. You're surely a thing to welcome any novel species of perversion!

REGAL (as if QL had not spoken): How about twenty-five follow-ers? That's plenty!

Her face brightened at her own genius touch.

QL: You make me mad, child.

She took hold of herself. Literally. She wrapped her arms over her chest and gripped her arms.

QL: I gave you everything and all.

LOVELY (muttering): In your own sweet time you gave it.

QL: I made you my guardians, my depositories. And now you would take all from me. But how now, Regal. You say I must keep five and twenty. Is that right?

REGAL: Yes, madam. Twenty-five.

Regal preened at Lovely, at Regal Consort, that she would be the one to set the bar.

QL: Well. Everything's relative, as the Old Earth texts would have it. When both are ugly, choose the one less ugly. Lovely, I and my fifty go with you.

REGAL: Mother—

LOVELY: Good, madam. What need you followers, after all? My staff is well-trained and plenty. Is it not enough?

Considering our unkempt quarters, the answer was clearly no. But that was hardly the point.

LOVELY: You'll be comfortable and safe, I promise. If any dare slack or slight you, we'll take care of it.

QL: What do you mean, why need I followers?

My heart broke, that she would give in and seriously respond to Lovely's taunting invitation.

QL: Why need you the handsome suit you wear? Wouldn't a servant's gown function as well to cover your body and keep you warm in this pleasant domain?

REGAL: Mother, it's not—

QL: Even the drab smulkins who toil in the filthiest Works treasure more than their needs require.

The dialogue went on. And on and on. I have not the heart to recall it all. Happily, Lovely's bodyguards kept off the bold crowd that gathered nearby. They heard nothing but surely the sight entertained: QL flushed and furious, Regal alternating between hysterical tears and hysterical laughter, Regal Consort contemptuous, Lovely cool and calm and, to her credit, trying hard to end the encounter without an outright scuffle.

GENTLEMAN (to Fool, in gesture-language): Why does QL deign to pursue this quarrel? And why go anywhere? Here in Serene, she keeps whatever retinue she sees fit.

FOOL (in gesture-language): Foolish friend. Is it not clear? Her mind is beclouded.

I began an objection, then subsided. What objection could be made? Her mind is beclouded. Truth.

A feeble jest flitted through my thoughts: are we not all beclouded, under this sky of ours, with its unending rain?

To be beclouded or not to be beclouded: it matters not for little folk such as Fool and me. Let us get unhinged! They will then put us away. End of story. QL's mental disorder, however, may lose us all Serene.

The Regals present little threat. Their sole interest in Serene is to drain its coffers to fund their lifestyle. Emoluments for bogus offices would placate them.

Lovely is of a different, more dangerous ilk. Her drug is pomp and power. Winning Serene, the last vestige of QL's Dominion, would be all the more sweet to her, as vengeance for QL slighting her and her sister (not that she cares about Regal) in favor of Princess, and for forcing her into a marriage she did not desire. There may also be some darker vendetta. She has pressed the claim that as a young maiden she endured some sordid abuse, and that QL did not protect her. QL denied it, even scoffed at her.

I do not know.

The plain fact is, even with the full count of her following, QL will fall if Lovely combines with Regal against her. United, their knights, led by Lovely Consort, would prevail, and the governors might well follow suit, with QL's dubious "deed" of Serene at their backs.

All this would wrap up the motive for the murder. Had Princess got back into her mother's good graces, bringing with her FR's alliance, any ambition Lovely held for Serene would have been thwarted forever.

And yet… Would Lovely have had her own sister killed? Would Regal? I can believe it of Regal Consort. Or the killer's commissioner could have been anyone, after all, who feared FR's influence swelling. It demanded neither patriotism nor great imagination to see that his ascendancy could depose many of rank.

At long last, QL broke away. Not surprisingly, no agreement had been reached as to where she would go and with how many followers. I hoped this meant she and her knights would stay here in Serene, immovable.

I resolved to speak with QL not as a mere spy, but, for the first time, as a counselor.

End of entry.

・・・

I DO NOT know what to do.

The usual. I shall try to straighten things up in my mind. Setting down a narration, I pray, will help me find the next step.

Back to where I left off—back to when things still, more or less, made sense. Though I hardly thought so at the time! Before my world turned inside out.

As we traveled back to QL's dismal quarters in frozen silence, I composed in my mind, grandiosely in retrospect, a report sound and reasonable. I rehearsed how to breech my usual reserve.

Madam, I think it my duty to advise… to warn….

Too forward.

Madam, may I venture to…

Madam, in my humble opinion…

Madam, it is my humble duty to infer…

On our arrival, with only a few befuddled servants in attendance, QL bundled herself up, willy-nilly, in waterproofs, armor, and furs, raving and ranting all the while.

QL: I'll meet him with some choice advice. Blow us down! Spit until you've drowned our domes.

Fool and I, huddled by the fish pool, managed to figure out that she was addressing, in her imagination, FR, as personified by the wild storm. Worse, she was going Outside to look for him.

QL: Drown those cocks who fuck our daughters—ha, who crack their nether cheeks, I'd warrant, for have those whores whelped us new heirs? Unleash ozone giants to cleave with their foul bolts the fair domes we built to withstand them—the domes that will soon withstand ourselves! Fear not to burn my white hairs out of my head. Only join high battle against those pernicious bitches who once were mine own daughters.

Fool—though I grabbed at its gown—bounded to grovel at her feet.

FOOL: Dear Madam, stay home, for this night's rising wrath will spare neither ruler nor your own poor Fool.

She heeded not the plea.

I emerged trembling to deliver my painfully rehearsed report, finishing by advising her (in timid and obsequious tones) to stay within, close to her own knights. Perhaps we could even quarter with them? What fun! We could have a nice party.

QL: Peace, little worm! Come not between the dragon and her wrath.

FOOL (daring to squeak on my behalf): Should duty dread to chastise majesty's folly?

QL (to both of us): Out of my sight!

My own life I never held dear. There is not much to make it dear, in fact, except Fool's friendship and a few pleasures—swimming around Serene, a drama well-conducted, eating certain foods. The pride and purpose of my life is to ward against QL's enemies by observing all. She has ever trusted me, ever relied on me, for this small duty. Never before has she sent me away, however unpleasant the news I relayed.

Humans cherish a difference, I learned today, between facts and truth.

As QL's company gathered in Serene's vestibule, bracing ourselves to brave the storm, Fool quietly implored me to stay Inside
and help Naphto set things right. Sometimes the cowardly course
happens to be most reasonable. I stayed Inside.

So, QL charged into a storm of record proportions escorted by
Fool and a couple dozen knights who looked to be scraped up from
the floor of a Naphta subDomain tavern. They might well have
been. Naphto supplied them and some stale rations, defying, to
his credit, Regal Consort's decree that QL should brave the storm
alone, with neither succor nor followers.

Wait! What of those hundred noble knights whose hand-
picked company QL so bitterly contested?

They, like me, stayed Inside, battle-grimed fingernails and all,
though not to "set things right" for QL.

One could hardly have expected otherwise. When soldiers
hold out their bowls, whoever pours into them money, shelter, and
victuals gains their fealty. Lovely now proudly claims her mother's
"blackguards" as her own.

End of entry.

• • •

2491.05.19.40

I HAVE NOT come close to helping Naphto set things right. When
I ventured to remind him, for example, that anyone of First Rank
can monitor the security vids in Serene's vestibule—meaning his
aid to QL may not have gone unobserved—he cut me off.

NAPHTO: Take heed, sirrah; the whip.

My skin splits deeply when beaten. QL never did it again, after
the first time. Among other factors, this prompted her to outlaw
physical contact, including corporal punishment, between humans

and smulkins. But this day, all defy QL, even her flabby minister, who responds to our crisis by pacing and wringing his hands.

I swear, if the deepest welts would dissuade my betters from the disasters on which they each and collectively embark, I would bear them gladly.

End of entry.

•••

2491.05.20.18

HABIT AND BOREDOM, not hope of utility, sent me forth this day on surveillance. My report follows. Not that anyone will receive it.

Item 01: This afternoon Lovely reviewed her newly enlarged army on the parade ground, the largest open space in Serene. I caught from them strains both of approval and of contempt, pretty much in equal measure. I admit, she is good with the men. She will soon have them in hand.

She wore her mother's ceremonial armor.

Item 02: Regal and Regal Consort celebrate what they perceive as their triumph over QL by drugging themselves to new highs—or lows, depending on how you see it. They are on amps and something else that puts a weird and dangerous light in their eyes. I would not cross them for my life.

Item 03: B-one Whoreson visited A-two True with the warning that Naphto suspects him of treachery. He did not describe the nature of this treachery, but A-two deduced that it involves an imaginary, long-simmering labor conspiracy. As if the workers have the wits, never mind the spirit, to stage a rebellion! It hardly matters. Since everyone suspects everyone of treachery, A-two swallowed whole his half-brother's half-truth as well as B-one's assurances that he would smooth things over with their mutual father.

B-one earnestly advised that, for his own safety, A-two must leave Serene for a while.

A-two would hardly have credited me, in his eyes an uppity flob, had I come forward to expose his bastard brother's deceit. He will be all right Outside, anyway, what with the training and equipment afforded by his expeditions. More important, he may find QL. She could use his help.

Item 04: No news from Lovely Consort, and my security medallion no longer accesses the e-room. By the way, signal to my audiopiece has been cut off, too.

Now do you see what I mean, about my world turned inside out? Everyone who should be Inside is Outside!

A poor clench, Fool would accuse. (Clench: an Old Earth term for a play on words that attains not even the lowly status of a pun.)

I returned from my information gathering foray—again, to what ends, I cannot say—to find Naphto engaged at his message console. When I called attention to myself, he made it clear he had no desire for my services or even my presence. I retreated to a dim corner.

Over the next couple of hours, he received a few messages to which he reacted with wordless vocalizations expressing both agitation and approbation. A burst of frenetic activity culminated in a message pod. I would have offered to deliver it, had he not immediately put in a call to B-one. In light of what soon followed, I believe he had forgotten my presence altogether.

B-one arrived promptly, surprisingly sober, and shaky and waxen as a result.

Naphto took no notice of his son's withdrawal symptoms. He did not even offer him a seat.

NAPHTO: My son, I like not these dealings. QL out in this storm, and not a finger lifted to prevent or persuade otherwise. Regal Consort threatened me with his displeasure, should I succor her, or insist she stay. How pitiless he was! And Regal with him. And Lovely, I suppose.

B-ONE: Savage and disgusting!

NAPHTO: Dangerously so. Listen. Regal Consort has summoned me, no doubt, to berate me for the small aid I gave QL—some provisions and an entourage of sorts, though hardly her best picked men.

B-ONE: You did well, father.

NAPHTO: I want you to report that I'm ill, to bed, that I cannot attend. The risk of surveillance dictates I must brave the storm to hand-post a message at Relay 10.3.

B-ONE: What message could be vital enough to send you into such wild hazard?

Naphto fingered the pod, hesitating, then divulged.

NAPHTO: Intelligence reveals that FR has advanced nearly within striking distance of Serene. This message… It begs that FR grant QL safe conduct to the comforts of his encampment, and that he seek a truce with Lovely Consort, whom I have reason to believe is displeased by the folly of this grief-induced campaign.

His compassion toward QL, and now this treasonous (though commendable) venture surprised me: dangerous and noble deeds for a man of his character.

B-ONE: This night is not for elders to brave.

NAPHTO: All goes exceeding strange, my son. An ozone giant was reported to have split into three. Large Moon shines dull red, the clouds ripping open some moments as if to display to our eyes the dolorous orb. This storm endures with a fury beyond record. Nature herself is at odds with us, and QL unsound…

B-one held out his hand.

B-ONE: Give the message to me, father. I'll take it to the Relay.

Naphto looked down at the pod, as if it would tell him what to do with it, then sighed, and handed it over.

NAPHTO: I pray you, be careful.

B-ONE: I will, father.

As B-one left, pod secured under his clothes, I wondered: would he redeem himself now? Have things gone too far, even for him? I could hardly believe it, yet the show was convincing. Even more convincing, on reflection: a treason conviction would strip Naphto of rank and estate, killing B-one's own prospects. Therefore, Whoreson would not betray his father. Still, my curiosity I followed; I tailed him.

Again, I underestimated B-one's powers of detection. I did not camo myself. In my defense, I assumed that, the parade ground being occupied, he would go by canal, and I would follow him underwater. Such are the hazards of having no audiopiece. He must have learned that Lovely's show was over; he suddenly turned toward the parade ground. Before I could find a discreet place to camo myself, he had spotted me. He beckoned me to him.

B-one: I should have known you would…. Go to my father. Stay by him.

I agreed, then tried again to tail him, this time in camo. Again, he spotted me and again directed me to return to Naphto's quarters.

End of entry.

. . .

NAPHTO DID NOT deserve his fate. My former contempt for him now lacerates me. Serves me right.

I returned to Naphto's quarters to find them unoccupied. After an hour or more wasted searching the vids, I took up his scent trail. Though faded, it remained distinctive enough: a bit sour and at the same time over-cleansed.

I caught up with him in a filthy knights' kitchen, disused this hour, yet glaringly lit. The Regals were in there, too. I crept in and hid under a prep table. (A habit: concealed observation. What I should have done was run for help—run anywhere.)

The following impressions, so wordy in my mind's record, in reality crashed by. Think in terms of thunderclaps. Moments of shattering terror.

A low villain with dirty hands held Naphto in a chair. The Regals stood facing him.

NAPHTO: What mean your graces? What foul play would you make on me?

REGAL CONSORT: Stinking fox. (To Villain): Bind him.

REGAL (to Villain): Hard, hard!

REGAL CONSORT: O filthy traitor!

NAPHTO: I'm none.

Oh, he looked so frightened, pinioned hand and foot to the chair.

Regal darted forward and yanked hard at his beard. He cried out. She came off with a handful of his gray hairs!

Naphto (eyes streaming): By the kind gods! To rob my face so saucily!

Regal: Where is my lunatic mother? Speak.

I do not know what I would have done—maybe nothing, maybe something—had a hand not suddenly clapped over my mouth and an arm seized my body.

It was Villain. So absorbed had I been in the horrible drama playing out before me, I had not noticed him creep around to join me under the prep table.

Villain (barely above his breath): One word, no' but a sound, and we both die.

I nodded; he eased his hand but kept it close to my face, at ready to silence me.

Regal (to Naphto): Answer!

Naphto: Unnatural daughter! Even refuge with our enemy will improve on the indignities her majesty suffered under this very dome.

Had he but answered their question literally and truthfully he might have saved himself! The literal truth being: he had no idea where she was! I am certain they did not intercept the message he had entrusted to B-one; they did not flaunt it or go to the point of it. He could even have boasted of what they knew already anyway, that he'd supplied her with rations and an escort. It would have given them something to gnaw. But his paranoia-induced and pathetic half-confession thrust him into deeper danger.

Regal Consort (with a gloating smile): Come, sir, you confess an exchange with FR?

NAPHTO: Nay! I—I… I messaged only a neutral.

Again, he needlessly betrayed himself!

REGAL: Cunning.

REGAL CONSORT: And false. Confess your confederacy with those who war on this—

REGAL: Where did you send her? (To Regal Consort:) Let him first answer that.

NAPHTO: To those who would cherish her.

REGAL CONSORT: Were you not charged at peril—

REGAL (SHRIEKING): Where?

NAPHTO: To FR! Yes! Because I would not see thy cruel nails scratch out her eyes nor your fangs sink into her anointed flesh. I pay penance now, for letting you lock Serene against her! But I shall be redeemed, to see her return in triumph with a true ally.

REGAL CONSORT: You'll see no such thing.

He grabbed the chair and tipped it until it fell over, and Naphto with it, the back of his head bouncing hard on the cement floor. Then, then—o how can humans adore gods who allow such things—then he grabbed a roasting spit and drove its point straight into Naphto's eye!

NAPHTO (screaming): Help! O cruel! O gods!

I sprang up, to be pulled back so hard my arm nearly left its socket.

VILLAIN (hissing in my ear; hand again clamped over my mouth): Stay, weakling!

REGAL (to Regal Consort, giggling): My love, look you. The eye remaining will mock its brother's poor, empty socket.

REGAL CONSORT (chuckling): How unkind. Let us take out the lousy thing.

He had dropped the spit; he rummaged in a drawer for another tool.

REGAL CONSORT (holding up a pair of tongs): This?

He rummaged again.

REGAL CONSORT (holding up a serving fork): Or this?

Struggling in Villain's clutches, I begged (biting the hand that would gag me) Regal Consort to withhold his hand, for his own good if not for mercy's sake. For my pains, Villain shoved a stinking dishrag into my mouth. He hardly needed bother. Had they noticed us, true, they would have killed us on the spot. But their sadistic sport utterly enthralled them, their shrieks of glee drowning any of my whimpers that escaped the gag.

VILLAIN (muttering): I'll never care what wickedness I do, if those two enjoy a long life!

I writhed and choked and whined, but I might have been a lobster being readied for the pot, for all the notice Villain took. A kick I landed on his knee finally served to make him aware of what he had hold of.

VILLAIN: A flob, valorous! You shame me.

He threw me aside, then sprinted from under the table, grabbing a chair leg broken off and rolling on the floor. Regal screamed warning as Villain raised his makeshift club. Regal Consort whirled about, drawing his own weapon.

Villain swung the club full round. Regal Consort fired him in the chest. But the chair leg connected—*crack!*—right upside Regal Consort's head.

Villain's good deed, his last—may flights of angels sing him to his rest!—came too late. Amidst the fury, Regal had clawed out Naphto's other eye. She raised it now, squinting.

REGAL (to Regal Consort, I think): Look! It's like a gross glob of jelly.

NAPHTO (groaning): O cold darkness.

Regal tossed away the eye to gaze smiling at her and her husband's handiwork: the agonized man. Meanwhile, Regal Consort staggered in a circle, vomiting, like a drunken dog chasing its tail. His wife finally noticed.

REGAL: What's with you?

REGAL CONSORT (clutching at her): I'm hurt, you stupid bitch!

Regal dabbled her fingers in the blood sheeting his temple. No shock, had she lapped it up.

REGAL CONSORT: Get me to a doctor!

They left the kitchen's disorder without even a glance at me. I worked the gag out and crawled to Naphto, still bound to the chair.

The only sound was my sobbing breath and Naphto's groans. The good Villain lay dead in a pool of blood, his chest blown clear open.

The battered furniture. The reek of blood and burnt flesh. And kitchen garbage.

I labored over the knots—they were well made—until the

idea occurred to me: we are in a place full of knives. I grabbed a stout blade and cut the bonds. I could hardly bear to look at the blood-filled pits that once cupped his pearly eyes. The remains of his beard stuck to his chin in bloody tatters.

I looked up to see two Servants staring from the doorway. I wondered how long they had stood there, gawking. Why had they not tried to stop this bloody mayhem.

GENTLEMAN: Whip up five egg whites.

A trick learned on campaign: egg whites stop blood.

They did not move. I whipped the egg whites myself, and applied them to Naphto's eyes. Where his eyes had been, I mean. At some point, the two Servants disappeared.

The Regals no doubt chose this kitchen for having a loading dock overlooking a midden, for ease of dumping Naphto Outside. All for the best. I managed to get him to his feet, and together we staggered through the bay.

By myself, I could have hidden somewhere Inside, but not with this burden, namely, Naphto. So an old blind man and I found ourselves, like everyone else I have ever trusted, thrust into the storm with little provision, no vehicle or shelter, and no means of navigation.

End of entry.

• • •

2491.05.20 OR 21

YET THE RAIN it raineth every day. With a hey-nonny-nonny-no!

Thus runs one of Fool's ditties through my mind. He sang it on a merry night, at banquet for QL's victorious return from some battle or other. Its humor lies in its origin: a musical set on Old Earth, where, they say, the rain did not raineth every day.

It always has, in my life, rained. Every day, and every night, too, with no letting up, though tonight it surely pelts down harder than anyone has ever known. And our shelter, an abandoned dome. My obscure suckling place could not have been much colder, drabber, harsher. Long forgotten, that teeming, filthy nest, and long gone into the jungle—good riddance, whatever B-one may say of a "snug and tidy den."

QL gave me shelter, clothes. She dried me! Her people taught me to speak, to think, to put my senses in order.

That was not why they took us, I have to admit. I would have been placed in a Works, had luck not made me Princess's pet.

I know how that sounds.

As she gave up childish pursuits, they separated us, but again luck posted me not in a Works but in the cemetery. Most lucky of all: the job threw Fool and me together. From there, we both rose to places in QL's court.

Maybe my assimilation spared a few others of my kind from life in a Works, showing as it did that smulkins possess human-like nature.

I once shared this thought with Fool—on the occasion, in fact, of chopping up QL's predecessor, a man deposed ere I was brought Inside. He died, QL's news agency had reported, by an accidental overdose of fun-chem.

With blade fresh-sharpened, Fool whacked off the head, then held it up, as if to admire its sunken, mottled flesh.

FOOL (to Head): I'll have you know, my human friend, that my smulkin friend here saved all of smulkin-kind!

Getting into the spirit of the jest, I mock puffed myself up.

GENTLEMAN: Always I knew myself to be cast in a heroic mold!

FOOL (to Head): Were it not for his humanish mold, my moldy

human, ere long we flobs would have ended up (grabbing Head's jaw and making him "chew") supplying First Rank's finest banquets.

GENTLEMAN: And smelt so delicious?

FOOL: Pah!

It tossed Head into the pit.

FOOL: The rogue died so corrupt, his corpse barely held together for the laying in.

Thus, Fool. One moment merry, the next bitter and melancholic.

I hope my friend is all right.

As for myself—alas! I may have avoided the serving platter, but a slot in a Works would vastly improve my present situation. The ozone giants conceal us for the time being, disrupting signals of drones and cyber hounds. But once the storm lets up, Regal and her Consort will surely take up the hunt. If B-one seeks his father…. He won't. If he learns of Naphto's absence at all, easier to tell himself, belike, that A-two will take care of him.

The gods who preside over the fate of humans did at least grant shelter to the old man and me. Whether they did so to prolong their sport or to mix a drop of mercy into the torrents of rain that fall, I surely do not know. Rude pylons raise our refuge high enough to keep out the most brazen fungi and flora. The smoggy dome leaks streams, but withstands the worst of water and wind. I grabbed some rations from the kitchen stores, on the way out.

This affords me a chance to put things in order.

I crouch in a filthy wigwam with two even more wretched than myself, one eyeless and moaning in a stupor of despair, shivering only a little less with my gown wrapped shawl-wise around him; the other gabbling in some mad language only he understands, his clothes so ragged they are more lattice than cover. Yes, we found squatting here a muttering madman (whose smell I cannot quite place, though it is disturbingly familiar).

And I prate of putting things in order.

Well, why not. It is not as if there is anything else to do.

On second thought—what do we do when we need mental respite? We seek entertainment! I will have to make my own, though. It will be an historical drama; it will take place when Princess still lived. One act is all that is needed. One scene will do it.

THE TRAGEDY OF QL

INTERIOR. THE BASILICA, Serene Dome. Afternoon.

At the center of the Basilica is the Round Table. Various knights, courtiers, and functionaries, including Archivist with scroll, Gentleman and Fool, attend.

A flourish. All stand.

Enter, in pairs: Naphto and FR Nobleman; Lovely and Lovely Consort; Regal and Regal Consort; Princess, covered in a thick, enveloping gown and head veil in the manner of FR's realm, and a Valet.

A flourish.

Enter, side by side, QL and FR. They stand by two chairs set at the Table, flanked by…

Dear heavens. Already the audience dozes off.

In real life, not one in that assembly would have dozed off. We all were on edge.

How do dramatists do it? They rely on actors. Yet how would actors convey the tension? A bunch of noble people stroll up to a big table. Big deal.

From the audience's point of view, the Princess would have been but a column of cloth. Not a she or a he, not young or old. They would not know that the nuptials of Princess and FR

Nobleman were to crown the festivities celebrating the new peace. They would not feel the sadness I communicated in gesture to Fool, as my hopes to see Princess's face, one last time, were dashed. Fool's and my secret language of gestures would mean nothing to an audience. Nothing at all. Merely background twitches made by a few domestics.

Strike fidgety courtiers!

Obviously, my talent lies in composing surveillance reports, not in conjuring drama. Besides, what is a drama without actors but a dry bone: no flesh, no blood, no life. No kind of entertainment.

QL knew the players, and their agendas and relations; she knew the setting; she knew what had gone before the scene, what had led up to it. She had lived—and made the history of it all. So, in her mind, my reports took on life. They became historical drama. Though I doubt she saw it that way.

Knew. Lived. Saw.

Past tense.

It needs to be set down. I will do it still: a tragedy, though not for the stage.

THE TRAGEDY OF QL

ACT I

FR AND AN entourage of his close retainers came in pomp to Serene to ratify a long-negotiated peace. The entire realm celebrated, for the treaty would end a war waged since time out of mind. The knights mourned not, either, for QL promised them new campaigns in new terrain, which meant, as Fool pointed out, new rank and new booty. All the better, for not being hemmed in by FR's nimble and potent armies.

The ceremony was to take place in the Basilica, an ingenious structure of interwoven trusses. Its brilliant decoration had been commissioned for the occasion of QL's accession. Our Ranks, in costume beautifully colored and richly textured, were Naphto, Lovely and Regal, and their consorts. And Princess. The courtiers craned to see from benches set at a decorous distance. Fool and I enjoyed nearer seats.

I had hoped Princess would name me her escort. Instead, a valet stood by her. Guided her, rather, a bit of her sleeve pinched between his fingers. Her fiancé, FR Nobleman, kept his place among FR's retainers. A minister equal in rank to Naphto, he held a subDomain that rivaled Naphta subDomain in monetary value.

How drab FR's entourage looked, in their well-cut gowns of sober black and brown. And Princess all the more drab, enveloped and veiled as she was from head to toe.

The making of the Basilica's Round Table, at which they gathered, cost three men's lives, its top a slab of real stone quarried from the Barren Plain and honed to satiny refinement.

(You see? Another detail I could not have put in a drama. From the audience's point of view, it is a big, heavy looking table. As part of a stage set, it would be something light-weight, shaped and painted up to look like stone. Or they might not even bother to reproduce the Round Table. In a drama, it could be any table, for none needed to know the real table's cost. And the Basilica's echoing grandeur would be sorely diminished as a set, even on the stage of the Royal Circus itself. And yet… A guilty shame touched me at the time, that the Basilica might seem to our visitors a bit tired, a bit old-fashioned. Frumpy, even. And our costumes not splendid but gaudy.)

Naphto gave a speech, going on at some length, and winding up at last with:

NAPHTO: We will no longer hamper each other, in realizing our mutual manifest destiny: to subdue this planet that is our home.

Fool (to Gentleman, in gesture-language): Our, meaning, belonging to humans.

Gentleman (to Fool, in gesture-language): Exactly. Our home.

The Archivist, on QL's signal, stepped forward and began to unroll, slowly, slowly, the scroll he had in hand. QL more or less shoved him aside, snatched the document, and snapped it open.

The edges ripped. But that's not what prompted the gasps and murmurs. The document was not a fancy script version of the Treaty, as we had assumed. It was the Map of QL's Succession.

QL: I have called you together to express a dark purpose.

Courtiers glanced covertly at each other, a whiff of apprehension rose. The silence stretched long enough for me, and each and every other person there, I am sure, to speculate on what might be this "dark purpose," on an occasion prepared for joy. Surely she would not renounce the Peace, all of a sudden.

QL: Know that, henceforth, we shall make our abode with each of our daughters in due turn, month by month, with reservation of one square of our best knights.

Puzzling, unsettling, and wildly out of step with the occasion, thought I, but not dark.
Then she continued.

QL: Our Dominion we shall deed separately to each of those daughters, that the younger ones may rule while the elder crawls nicely to death.

Heart pounding, I breathed deep, yet discerned no cause of imminent death upon her. She is a most vigorous and virile woman.
Fool, more discerning, or less gob-struck, drew in breath not to take a scent but maybe to mock and rail into the yawning

silence—but a look from Lovely made clear, it would not do. Anyway, as we would learn, no wit would have prevailed where reason itself failed to brook QL's purpose.

Her weighty intention she had kept shrouded, pitch dark indeed, from all, for she surely knew that her loyal followers would have stopped at nothing to stop her. Nearly unwise as the deed, not to mention the embarrassing timing of it, was the manner of its doing. The shattering of her realm—the realm she had seized with cunning and valor, the realm whose domains were kept solid in this watery World of ours by the blood and labor of many a human and smulkin—she crafted as a tournament of toadyism.

QL: Which of my daughters loves me most, I wonder? Who should have the best of my Domains?

Lovely and Regal kept a demure silence, probably waiting for the other to speak so she could outdo her. Princess, too, kept silent. As future consort to FR's minister, she would happily have assumed herself excluded from the contest, for however tight the Peace Treaty might turn out to be, QL would surely never place "the best of her domains"—namely Serene and Domain 2—so intimate to the grasp of our ancient enemy. The territory in Princess's dowry was Domain 3. Its oculus depleted, its Works played out, its only virtue lay in straddling an old border disputed with FR. Its inclusion among the riches that Princess would bring her husband was merely a courtesy to her fiancé's lord.

QL: First you, eldest.

LOVELY: Madam, I cannot express how much I love you.

Ambiguous as those words could be read, QL drew another gasp from the assembly, and a whimper from the archivist, by boldly writing on the map, over Domain 02: "LOVELY"

QL: What say you, next daughter?

Regal smirked and simpered, while her consort positively glowed: Serene was all but theirs, so they would have thought. Fool's and my hearts sank at the prospect of Serene falling into the hands of QL's least-witted daughter—or rather, the greedy paws of that daughter's consort. Naphto looked less than enthusiastic himself.

QL: Regal? How now?

Regal Consort muttered something in his wife's ear.

REGAL: My dear elder sister can only hint at the very deed of my love, and…

Another whispered prompt.

REGAL: Oh! And I must add that I profess myself an enemy to all other joys but you, Mother Dear!

I sensed Fool just about bursting to put in that her recreational habits certainly displayed no enmity to other joys, but it managed to hold its too agile tongue.

There, however, the contest did not end. QL did not reward such brazen flattery with Serene. She turned to Princess.

QL: And you, my youngest? What say you?

Princess, included in this game! Her fiancé drew himself up, his eyes gleaming bright at the largesse Princess might now, unexpectedly, bring to their marriage. Fool and I, too, foolishly and silently rejoiced. Princess might rule Serene after all, if….

If.

If she would better, or merely echo, her sisters' professions.

At the time, to be honest, neither Fool nor I even considered an "if." We assumed that whatever Princess said would win the day, and win Serene. She had always been, without question, QL's darling.

She said not a word. Her silence disconcerted us, underlined as it was by the all-concealing garments.

QL (playfully): Come on. Nothing comes of nothing.

Inwardly I seconded QL's urging. Come, my Princess, speak your heart.

My prayer was answered. But, alas, I forgot in making it, the gods do practice cruel jests on their subjects.

Princess did finally speak, her voice, as ever, soft, gentle, and low, and somewhat muffled by the veil.

Princess: I must love most who will be my husband.

Given the presence of her affianced, I thought (a touch desperately), and her affianced's lord FR, the answer was only diplomatic. Then she added, unfortunately:

Princess: I shall never marry like my sisters, to love my mother all. My husband, with whom I shall share my fortune, will have his due share of my heart.

Fool gibbered something, I think to distract, or to put things on another track—anything to head off what was coming, what was clearly coming, for a certain kind of smoke and darkness wrapped QL. I had seen it before. On a battle's loss, for example.

FR Nobleman pursed his lips. Though not made like me, he too sensed that Princess's words were not such to win a rich domain.

QL: So young, and so untender?

Please, my Princess, I begged inwardly, play the hypocrite this once, with so much at stake!

Princess: So young, madam, and so true.

QL: So be it, girl. Your truth shall be your dowry.

A few moments of silent confusion passed as all parsed the apparent violation of the prenuptial agreement. Then a murmur broke forth, quickly stifled by decorum. FR Nobleman looked to his lord, to QL, to Princess. He resembled nothing more than a confused dog. FR himself stood unperturbed in expression, yet wreathed in a honeyed, salty scent I could not at the time fathom.

QL: My true daughters, Lovely and Regal, and their consorts shall digest the portion of my realm that would have gone to the one there, that stranger to my heart.

She wrote on the map "REGAL" over Domain 03, then faced FR Nobleman. (Note, she did not mark Serene in any way, nor name it aloud.)

QL: We excuse you, sir, with no ill will, from the engagement that once brought us such joy. Let the maiden take upright pride to her cold bed.

While she thus deeded two of her three domains to Lovely and Regal, along with, very arguably, Serene Domain, Princess stood silent, hidden beneath the veil. I know she wept, though. Her tears I smelled, her gentle sobs I heard. How I longed to run to her, that she would take me up in her arms, as in days of yore, when I comforted her out of childish woes. She did not, at the conference, even have by her the little dog that had taken my place.

FR took her… I think, by the hand, and led her to face Nobleman.

FR: Will you not take this maiden for your own? She is herself a dowry.

FR Nobleman (blushing dark): I am sorry that even as she loses her mother she loses her future husband.

FR (softly): Not so, not so.

FR Nobleman: The promise made to me is broken, sir.

FR: Yes. The promise made to you is truly broken.

Princess drew herself tall and raised the veil covering her head. How beautiful her face, tear-stained though it was!

Princess (to FR Nobleman): I am no more sorry to lose a fortune-seeker than such a one is to lose an undowered bride.

FR Nobleman solemnly nodded, as if to say, fair enough, but with no relenting on his part.

FR (to FR Nobleman): You relinquish this woman?

FR Nobleman: With regret, I do relinquish my part in this broken agreement.

FR (smiling, to Princess): Then I do take you, and your virtues I seize as your dower.

Princess stared at him, then bowed her head. Gently, FR raised her chin and tenderly kissed her tear-wet lips, then lowered the veil again over her.
I was blown away.

FR (to FR Nobleman): Too bad, waterish man, you have lost forever this precious outcast, now queen of my realm.

FR left that very day, taking our Princess and leaving behind the shattered prospects of peace.
Who could blame him for abandoning, unsigned, the treaty

so painstakingly negotiated? QL's rash upheaval of the status quo hardly boded well for keeping faith with any kind of agreement. Besides, if he took up arms again, he would no longer contend against the entire might of QL but against a realm divided. He could seize it, domain by domain. (In fact, he started right away, by demolishing the border Domain before Regal had a chance even to hang new drapes in its moldy palace. She repines not, though she is pleased to keep its rank.)

It could be that in taking Princess, FR banked on QL changing her mind, restoring the dowry, and handing over Serene in the bargain. Whatever the mix of his purpose, I say his deed was nobly done. Fool and I, discussing it later, decided that the strange, delicious, salty-sweet odor was the essence of human love.

However skillfully I may have discerned the mix of FR's motives, I could not catch even a glimmer of the reason, or of reason itself, behind QL's umbrage at Princess's obvious sincerity, clumsily put though it was. But what would I, Gentleman, know of the duty and love owed from mother to child and child to mother?

I did allow a timid, disloyal hope that, in the fateful hour, the newly affianced couple would take me away. That Princess would declare she could not possibly leave me behind.

She did not. I suppose she could not bring herself to separate me from my friend and my only home, or to rob her mother of my services, however modest they may be.

I belong to QL.

Loyalty.

Loyalty.

•••

THE SCRIPT WAS to read, at Princess's departure: *Exeunt.* But while *The Tragedy of QL* is well-launched, it draws not even close to its climax, let alone its end. This scene is more fitting as the first act only.

An act that ends poorly, for no one would be entertained by the musings of a sad little smulkin.

Strike smulkin's sad musings and, for that matter, Regal's mildewed prize. Let there be a more fitting end to the act:

FR left that very day, taking our Princess and leaving behind the shattered prospects of peace and a fractured realm.

ACT II.

No suspense on offer. You know what happened next.

When Princess brought new peace overtures to Serene, we were on campaign against a colony of gobbledeens whose predations were wreaking havoc on Lovely Domain's supply capsules. (I wonder, how "human" are they? Alas, there remains no Princess to find out.) Meanwhile, at Serene, Naphto, as QL's proxy, accepted Princess as FR's ambassador.

It hardly alleviates my pointless bitterness to consider that, first, it was not Lovely Domain's "due turn" to host us, and that, second, Lovely herself did not request, and probably did not need or want, our aid in repelling the raiders. In other words, we could have been at Serene when Princess arrived. Instead, while the oily blood of gobbledeen heads oozed down the spiked battlements of Lovely Domain, Princess was murdered at Serene Domain.

I do not know how that scene—the murder—was played out.

This, Act II, will also include the quarrels between QL and her daughters, and the intrigue B-one concocted. A nice parallel, a double-plotted play: two elders benighted and bewildered by their children.

ACT III.

Scene 1: QL wanders Outside in a record-breaking storm. The Fool harangues her, its way of spreading cheer. QL's escort, a sloppy bunch of tavern knights, straggles here and there, some drunk, others stupefied by the lightning and torrential rain.

This scene is, of course, pure fantasy. For all I know, every one of them could already have perished.

Scene 2: A dirty kitchen. QL's prime minister Naphto is bound to a chair, one eye socket empty. QL's daughter Regal and her Consort loom over him, their clothes blood spattered. Villain lies dead. Gentleman crouches under the table. (Would that I had not swelled that scene!) Regal plucks out Naphto's other eye.

Regal (holding up the eyeball, triumphant): Vile jelly! Where is your luster now?

Naphto: O cold darkness!

Yes, I know she did not say that. I am only trying to inject a little dignity into a sordid torture scene.

ACT IV (NOW)

If an ozone giant finds us, we are dead. If gobbledeens group an attack, we are dead. If the elements breech our shelter, we are dead. To paraphrase my poor friend Fool, wherever it might be: This night pities neither wise man—not that we have such in our company—nor this Gentleman.

Even our rainy, rainy world, the storm has swamped. Seeps have become ponds; ponds, lakes; puddles, marshes. My gills flex and twitch, abetting my urge to swim away. I could get both far and nowhere, swimming.

Aside from that, nothing is happening.

I suppose that makes this an interval, not an act.

• • •

2491.05; DAY AND HOUR UNKNOWN

THEY ROAM TOGETHER, Naphto and Madman, within our ramshackle dome. They seem to have forgotten me, and I do nothing to remind them of my existence.

The urge to leave continues to nag. After all, the old man now has another guardian, or at least the company of a fellow human who does not bear him malice and who possesses the will to live. Is it enough? Pity I have in plenty for Naphto, but he is not my job. I need to find QL. Besides, I fear Madman. Not because he is mad, but because of a creeping certainty that he is not mad. That he is acting. Which means, it would be wrong to abandon Naphto to him.

He guides the old man through an imaginary Old Earth terrain, with enormous hard-stemmed plants, expanses bare of vegetation, extreme protuberances and vast depressions.

MADMAN: Look how we labor up this hill.

NAPHTO: A hill?

MADMAN: Do you hear the torrent?

NAPHTO: Yes! Yes, I hear it.

So do I hear the torrent but not the one Madman hears, or pretends to hear. He refers to an Old Earth feature called a waterfall. We do not have them. Though they say this World is spherical, for all intents and purposes, it is flat. Except as rain, water does not "fall," as in a fountain or from a spout. It does not even flow, really. It pools. The torrent we hear is rain cascading over, and in spots pouring into, our cut-rate dome.

I also hear that Madman's way of speaking has changed. He grows more coherent.

The overlays of scent that express moods and emotions can be covered or confused by crafty perfumes. But at base, every living body emits an odor as distinct as the pattern incised on a human's fingertips. Plus, my memory is perfect. This means, no scent of human, smulkin, or animal, can be both familiar and unidentifiable to me. Yet the Madman's scent is both.

What is he?

MADMAN: From here, a river hurls itself over an edge so fearful, it turns my brain. An ozone giant stalks below, a mere spark in the abyss. How fearful! It makes me dizzy just to look!

NAPHTO: Let me see.

Madman takes Naphto to the brink of his completely fictional edge, then crouches behind him. At least I need not worry about him pushing the old man from a height!

MADMAN: Nothing under our broken moons would tempt me closer to this extreme verge. Take but a few more steps, and down you go into oblivion.

NAPHTO: Leave me here, friend. Wait, take this purse. In it, find your due for being my faithful guide. May it prosper you!

He hands the madman a purse—hands him nothing, in other words, for his purse was snatched by Villain, whom it certainly did not prosper.

NAPHTO: No harm or help can I ever do again in this World. I can only suffer. Let it end.

He then "jumps." That is, he flops on his face.

Madman turns out to be as I suspected: no kind of madman at

all. He now takes the guise of a farmer, come across Naphto at the edge of some pool "dug out by the cataract." By an elaborate and imaginary recreation of Old Earth, he assures the old man that he just fell from a great height and survived. But wait! The fantastical ruse comes to a wonderful end. He convinces Naphto that, by the miracle of being spared the "horrid crime of self-murder," it is incumbent on him to live.

I creep closer, to try again the scent of this noble "farmer."

FARMER: Upon the crown o' the cliff, what was the thing with you?

NAPHTO: A madman, I think. Though his rants hardly made less sense than some I've lately heard.

FARMER: No man, and not human. It had eyes like two full moons, snouts galore, and ridgy, bending horns.

NAPHTO: Yes… Yes! It was a flob! Those snouts…

I suppose we could seem like that, to humans. Yet no other smulkins have I detected here.

FARMER: This fiend it was that brought you to a brink and inspired the leap that should have been the death of you, but for the mercy of the gods.

NAPHTO: Ah! That foul smulkin, that cursed flob! It's harried me for days now! Halloo, halloo, loo, loo! My own sons, it turned against me. It wielded the device that blinded me!

FARMER: The smulkin blinded you?

Startled, Madman/Farmer falls out of character, and it comes clear in a flash: He is A-two!

And the "foul smulkin" is me!

Naphto (in a mumbling sob): Upon my eyes it feasted…

I cannot believe… I must—

•••

2491.05 (DAY AND HOUR UNKNOWN)

I know I am in Naphta subDomain. My "ridgy, bending horns" (not horns, but rather the smulkin equivalent of human ears) are pierced by industry's screams and screeches, whistles, howls, buzzing whines, crashes, clanks, bangs. The fumes invading my "snouts galore" (one nose with four nostrils, to be exact) burn my "eyes like two moons" (correct enough: I have two large, pale eyes).

Three solid walls and a fourth wall of metal netting confine me. I know not if it is night or day; the light stays on all the time. I cannot sense any other prisoners. It is chilly. No one returned or replaced my gown that wrapped Naphto. Welts from being bound ladder my arms. Thank the lesser gods who look over smulkins, A-two did not tether me by the neck!

I should have abandoned Naphto… When? Sooner. Much sooner. How could I not have recognized A-two right away? Who else would have the talent to brew such an all-baffling perfume? Had I known it was him, I would have fled, leaving Naphto to his care.

On second thought, no, I would not have fled. I would have let myself be known. Little as we like each other, I would not have guessed he would believe his gibbering father's wild accusations against me.

His father's word, against mine. A man, versus a flob.

Seriously?

But… Naphto turning on me with such ugly slander.

What…

What's happening?

Such are the useless thoughts that keep me occupied, in this lockup. The only certainty: the unstrained rain of mercy that the gods drop, now and then, upon their human subjects has not yet dropped upon this Gentleman.

The jail guards, formerly soldiers in QL's late campaign, speak not with me, but they do chat in my hearing. It is a kindness they give; I was something of a mascot to the troops. Or, given my absolute powerlessness, they could not care less if I hear them.

From what news they let fall, several threads can be knit up.

Item 01: Our troops (ie, Lovely Consort's army) made no belligerent engagement with FR. More to follow.

Item 02: Lovely Consort brought QL back to Serene and, according to his news agency, "ensures she receives all the comforts and dignity her late eminence deserves." Rumor claims he found her wandering half-naked and raving in the storm. Of her ragtag entourage, only Fool stayed by her. For such courage and loyalty, my friend stands accused of crafting her demise.

Item 03: In other smulkin news, I am accused (in the court of rumor; to my knowledge, no formal charges have been brought) of gouging out Naphto's eyes. The testimony of those servants who stumbled into the kitchen after the atrocity damns me. There I was, covered with blood, clutching a knife, stooped over Naphto's empty eye sockets.

Salt shaker in my other hand? (Re, the additional rumor of me eating the eyes.)

Not a jest to set the table on a roar.

I have no advocate. Maybe QL tried to defend me, to no avail; the testimony of a woman judged insane would carry no weight. No one has, apparently, pointed out that I have not the strength to do what they accuse me of doing. If a knight or two ventured to opine something like, the little flobbie was always so meek and mild, they would follow up with, I never would have thought it had this in it.

What took me so long to realize what I am, among humans?

Never mind. It is plain enough. QL's shelter blinded me to myself.

Anyway.

Item 04: Regal Consort died of the head injury dealt by Villain.

Item 05: Regal and Lovely killed each other. Rumor has it, they quarreled over B-one's affections. That could well be, but to the death? Not Lovely, at least. My guess, for what it is worth, is that in some crazed impulse Regal attacked, Lovely defended, both lost.

Lovely Consort, sporting a black armband, claims that "duty permits me not the mourning proper to my late wife." He is a big man now, you see. Everything is his.

Everything.

It is tempting to deduce he plotted all this, but informed instinct says, no, he only seized the day.

I suppose this deserves its own item.

Item 06: KL's coronation ceremony, lavish yet tastefully subdued, took place as hastily as pomp and propriety allowed, "the gored realm to sustain," as he said in his accession speech. FR attended, in his style of mourning. Veiled.

This being as good a spot as any to end *Traged*y of QL:
Exeunt.
Wait. Strike item 03. Because, who cares?
Exeunt.

• • •

2491.05 (OR 6?)

Item: Judging by current events, B-one did faithfully deliver Naphto's message, and he—he alone—does not lay his father's demise on one or another convenient smulkin. On the other hand, it does not seem to have occurred to him to redeem me. Easier for him to stay holed up in his palace, getting stoned and waiting for everything to blow over.

Item: A-two organizes a pogrom. The smulkins, you see, plot to foment homicidal insanity among the humans. Proof: Regal Servant's presence, at Lovely's and Regal's mutual murder. (Said smulkin was duly executed, btw.) After the humans slaughter each other, we will eat them. The guards find the whole thing laughable, joking about not daring to turn their backs on "the little one," that is, me. Given my continuing solitude, they must be killing them— killing us, that is—outright, versus rounding us up.

Item: Naphto died. I suppose that should be included in The Tragedy of QL.

Not worth an item but: no one has hurt me, beyond A-two's rough handling. I suppose I am being kept whole for a purpose. Some sadistic entertainment? At least it will not be the Regals heading it up!

I wonder if Fool made it to FR's camp. And if our new ruler KL protects it. Or if it is hiding low enough to be missed by A-two's grim reapers.

End of entry.

• • •

(DAY AND HOUR UNKNOWN)

THE SMELLS AND sounds in here bother me less. Not that they diminish. It's only that I grow accustomed to them. In literal fact, industry continues without pause.

Item: A-two's pogrom was a flop.

Only an idealist like him would think that a crusade to purge the domes of smulkins could gather adherents. Consider. When

QL took power, several rival (human) clans were subdued, chosen members of their families assassinated. The subsequent confiscations yielded armies, Works, palaces, treasuries.

Works "manned" by smulkins.

QL's ceremonial armor also came by way of the coup. Poor Lovely wore it but once, in the brief span of her triumph. Yes. Poor Lovely. She should have gotten Serene—she should have gotten the entire realm. She would have ruled well. I wonder what I might have done differently, had this clear insight come more timely. Or if my support would have made any difference.

Back to "Item," re A-two's pogrom. Of course it flopped. Nothing can be reaped from the corpses of the wretches who slave in the Works. Their only value is their labor. Thus, they are spared.

I cared little for the lowest of the low among us, when I trailed in the train of QL's pomp. The bitter pill, which I never took, would have been to go down amongst this realm's "flobs," to feel, even secondly, what they do feel. A visit to Works might have physicked my swollen head.

More likely, it would merely have shaken into their hands some coins of the small wealth granted me. A pittance toward balancing the pans of justice: some pity bestowed, and a few pennies.

I doubt I would have done more. To be honest.

End of entry.

• • •

My poor Fool, dead.

Guard 1: E'en her majesty's little critter, the joker, they cut down.

Guard 2: Now that's a pity.

They were, perhaps, among those that Fool kept a-roar with laughter, in happier times.

Will angels sing a smulkin to the happy palace of the dead?

I pray the end came quick.

• • •

Maybe when the Guards return from wherever they went, they will pass on more news "accidentally on purpose." I would love to get a clue or two about what will happen to me.

Or I could ask them, point blank: What am I being held for?

Hopefully, they will bring plenty of water, too. My skin is starting to crack.

• • •

Self-murder is a "horrid crime," A-two preached to his father. Murder and mayhem rule, yet we are not to end ourselves.

• • •

Once upon a time…

Some parents went off-nest to get provisions. Only three of their twelve children survived that day. Of those three, two died soon after, in captivity.

I alone live.

Why should a dog, a horse, a rat, have life, and my litter mates no breath at all?

• • •

I am hungry and thirsty. Very hungry and very thirsty.

My skin is a mess.

• • •

I think the humans have forgotten me.

•••

Exeunt.

••• •••

Sundowning

"Someone to watch over me," she sang.

She signaled left. Deliberately. Mindfully, rather.

It wasn't a symptom, singing to herself. She'd done it for years. After everything else slipped away, she'd probably still be plagued by bits and pieces of songs rambling around her head. Oldies only. Longterm memory, the doctor had told her, tends to endure longer.

She'd pretended to him that her sister, younger, devoted, lived nearby. But really, no one to watch over her. No real support system. Will gone. Steve and Julie gone. Dad and Mom long gone. Friends gone, or just drifted away.

She didn't regret not having had children. Except that after her memory disappeared, nothing would remain of Will. A few of her poetry books were still in print, but he, a plain, loving man, lived only in living memory. No children, no grandchildren to carry his life to the future, to inherit his wisdom and his few treasures: the pocket watch from his grandfather, a curious sea shell he'd harvested as a child from one of the barrier islands off North Carolina.

She drove very carefully, took her time. Having no children also meant no one to wrest away her driver's license, at least not until she made a mistake. Maybe a horrible mistake. No one to pry her from the cottage. No one to take ownership of her life.

Neighbors might check in. The family across the road. Good people.

She'd called the propane man last month and told him to take away the tank. She was going electric, she'd lied. The truth was, she'd called after finding one of the stove burners going with nothing on it. She used the microwave now. Aging in place.

A few nights ago, she woke for no reason that she knew. Got up and walked around the cottage, turning on lights—she'd known, somehow, where to find the switches. She looked at the furniture, the books, the artwork on the walls. Opened the linen closet and stared into it. Picked up a beautiful glass bowl and turned it in her hands.

It was all so familiar.

Finally, she sat on her screened porch in the dark and concentrated simply on not panicking. When she woke in the dawn, slumped on the dew-damp glider, everything was back to normal. The furniture, the books, the artwork. The Venetian glass bowl Will and she bought for their fortieth anniversary.

Things could never be normal again. She knew that. She tried to impress in her mind each landmark between her cottage and town: the big oak tree at the crossroads, the rail fence a half mile further on, the little cross that marked where the neighbor's boy missed the turn and flipped over. Sooner or later, though, she'd get lost. She'd gotten lost in her own house.

The odd thing was, while it happened she kept thinking, *if only Will were alive, he could tell me what this place is.*

Maybe she should contact social services, get someone to check in on her. But first she needed to find out what they could do to her. Put her in a county nursing home? Revoke her drivers license? Would a social worker take over her life? She considered herself well educated, but about her present situation she was as ignorant as could be. Deliberately ignorant. She'd thought she was being realistic, with the stove and other little compensations, but she'd refused to look squarely at the situation. Maybe if she had internet at home…. But she and Will had opted for freedom, quiet.

Back home, she hung her car keys by the door and went to her desk. She should keep a journal. Someone had done that. An article in the New York Times about it. An artist or intellectual. But writing had become an accusation of her condition. Thoughts didn't string together. Sometimes, just completing a cogent sentence. She opened her journal. The last entry was dated January 12th, about nine months ago.

A sensation she called shimmering simmering came over her body. She took refuge on the screened porch as she had so many times since Will died, tried to put her mind to mundane tasks. Warm up the leftover soup for dinner. When would she forget to turn off the stove? She should make sure the propane wouldn't run out. But it was delivered on schedule. The man out here last…. When?

The soft damp heat, the catalpa and pine shadow-lace cast by the setting sun, the cricket and frog song soothed her. She loved this place and didn't want to leave it. Not just for itself but because it contained her best memories of Will. They'd lived plenty of other places, but this sweet, beat-up little cottage amidst cotton fields and scraggly woods was what they called, tongue-in-cheek but for real, their dream home. No family ties, just cheap land, hoot owl lullabies, decent neighbors.

She should have set up automatic bill payments through the bank months ago. Why had she put it off? As if she needed a doctor's pronouncement. She'd go to the library, get them to help her. Right now. They were open 'til eight, weekdays. She went in the house again, methodically gathered her bills. And here was the missing checkbook, thank heavens.

She should record in her journal Will's and her life together.

Hoard memories against oblivion. But when her and Will's life together slipped so far away from her she could recall it only by reading words about it, that life, and the words about it would probably hold no meaning.

For now, the old memories lingered. It was the new ones, the necessary ones—what happened yesterday, last week, a few minutes ago—that betrayed her.

She clipped the bills together and stuffed them in her knapsack. Maybe it was a good thing she'd been absent-minded all her life. She already had systems in place to compensate, although it hadn't helped with the checkbook. She could always disconnect the range, just use the microwave. When, though? She grabbed her keys—nice habit, that hook by the door, and her purse from the coatrack.

At the foot of the driveway, she stopped the car to get the mail. Then she just sat, her hands on the wheel. She'd done it already. The propane. Last week? A man came and took away the tank. She took a deep breath. She had to get used to this, somehow. After gazing at the gear shift to make sure she'd put it in park, she got out of the car, looked both ways several times, and crossed the road to the mailbox. She reached into the box.

A sound like a shrieking intake of breath.

A pulsation of heat like a gigantic oven door opening.

Her ears rang. Envelopes scattered on the ground. She turned.

Smoke rose from behind the cedars along her fence.

She took a step, stopped, looked both ways, ran back across the road. At the bottom of the driveway, she stopped so hard, she almost fell over.

An incomprehensible scene lay before her. Like a Dali painting of Alzheimer's, a surreal hallucination. She couldn't figure it out. Or maybe it wasn't her; maybe it truly didn't make sense.

Where her cottage had stood, a flattish mound of debris

smoldered. Bluish flames licked up here and there. A ragged part of a kitchen wall remained. So did the gnarled catalpa, the loblollies, the crepe myrtles around the bird bath, even her little rose garden. The cinderblock garage. The basket of pine cones on the picnic table.

A bomb. A meteor. The propane tank.

Yet it wasn't like the aftermath of an explosion, with a wild scattering of crack-glassed photos, broken furniture, splayed open books, tangles of clothes: none of the homey fragments beloved by post-disaster TV reporters. The debris lay as a neat blanket of embers, ashes, and indiscriminate dark chunks no bigger than her two fists clenched together. And the partial kitchen wall, with the pots and pans on their rack, still swinging slightly, the cupboards hanging open, dishes tumbled out.

Slowly she realized nothing else was happening. No firetrucks screaming, no frantic neighbors. The thin pillar of smoke that rose could look, from a distance, like someone burning trash or leaves. Folks around here still did that. From the road, you wouldn't even guess what happened, the cedars lined thick along the old rail fence.

The most dramatic, or rather newsworthy event of her life had no audience, witness, commentator. Ludicrous. No, not ludicrous. She searched for what it was—a poet's habit, not a loss for words. Except she couldn't find the word.

Something had destroyed her cottage so instantly and completely, it hadn't even raised a cloud of dust and smoke. Had she been in inside, she would be part of that heap.

She'd been going somewhere. Her car idled at the bottom of the driveway. She'd stopped at the road, gotten out to check the mail. She remembered opening the box, but she couldn't remember if she'd taken out any mail. Well, surely she could be forgiven that much.

She went to her car, got in. She turned the key, raising a grating shriek from the already running engine. Sooner or later, she would lock herself out of her car. She would leave her purse, now on the seat beside her, at the bank, the library, the little diner where she ate lunch when she went to town.

All her photos, letters, manuscripts, gone. Her journal, her pens and pencils, her computer, gone. Her little collection of signed books, by friends and fellow poets. Will's nature books. Her own books, most out of print now. The Venetian glass dish. The towels and sheets, and the tablecloths from Mom that she never used—too much trouble to iron.

She pulled her purse onto her lap, looked inside. The bills weren't there. It didn't matter, but where had they gone? Were they among the ashes of the dictionary and thesaurus she'd kept on her desk? Her parents had given her the dictionary when she went to college. Her own dictionary with their loving inscription. Oh, how she missed her family.

Death. One of the four rivers of suffering the Buddha delineated: birth, old age, sickness, and death. She had a foot in two of the rivers. Now, like a forced leap toward her own demise, she'd had a huge chunk of her life torn away all at once. Literally, in a flash. Every material object she'd ever cared about, obliterated. She was lucky, though. What about old people in Afghanistan, Syria, the Congo? Her garage could shelter her, at least until winter, and she'd stashed canned food and jugs of water in there. So she was set.

She came out of her musings with a start. Why was she planning to hole up in her garage? Why not drive to town and tell someone—the police, the fire department—what happened? But as soon as the question arose, she knew the answer. She now feared authority. She didn't know what they would do with a solitary, senile old woman whose home most assuredly no longer met code, even in these parts. The doctor had said something about her living alone, hadn't he? He might think it his duty to report her to social services. Might be afraid not to, for that matter. No, the devoted sister who lived nearby. What if he found out the sister was really dead?

She could go to town and eat at the diner, try to figure out what to do. Call her insurance agent. Her friend Margaret. Had she paid her premiums? She should have used the library internet to set up automatic payments. She could still do it. Except all the paperwork was destroyed because somehow or other she'd stupidly removed the bills from her purse. Or never put them in there in the first place. She didn't even have anything to write with, because she must have taken out her notebook, too, and her pens and pencils.

No, everything was in her knapsack. She'd never put them in this purse at all. It wasn't the first time she'd done something like this, but it was the worst time. Even as the tears slipped from her eyes, she laughed.

"Not the first time, but the worst time. I'm a poet and don't I know it."

She turned on the car radio. Today, she could break the "no media before 5 p.m." rule. It was after 5, anyway. The classical station static, she switched to country. Grim voices replaced banal love songs.

"… not meteors," a man was saying, "nor any known armament."

"What do we know about them?" a woman asked. Clearly, she was the newscaster, he the expert.

"Each UHO is essentially a unit of extremely intense heat enveloped in such a way that the heat does not dissipate until the UHO strikes something solid. They seem to range in size from golf balls to, let's say, SUVs. So far, no traces of the envelope material has been recovered at the target sites. The affect is—"

The newscaster broke in. "Target sites? So you believe this is a targeted attack?"

"We are investigating all possibilities. Whatever the intention—if there is one—it is very unlikely that the UHOs were launched from anywhere on earth. Surveillance data from international satellites indicate no launches of the magnitude required for the scope of these strikes. In other words, we are virtually certain that the UHOs originated from outside our atmosphere."

The newscaster gave a little laugh both frightened and mocking. "Are you saying this is an invasion from outer space?"

"As I said, we are investigating all possibilities."

He seemed about to say more, but the newscaster hurriedly said, "Thank you, Dr. Phillips. Now to our correspondent Rob Snyder in Washington. Rob?"

Rob spoke in a rapid gabble that took a while to follow. Finally, she gleaned that UHO stood for Unidentified Heat Object, and that these UHOs were moving over the northern hemisphere east to west.

The destruction had started in Newfoundland. As the earth turned—like a chicken on a spit, she thought—the destruction advanced, dotting, so far, the United States and Canada. The hits seemed random, without strategy. In Washington, DC, the Phillips Collection utterly destroyed, while government buildings went unscathed. The Phillips Collection—with Renoir's *Boating Party*! Her father's favorite painting. A car in Wheeling, West Virginia, with a hole clear through it. New York, 9/11 all over again. A Kansas wheat field sheeted in flame. A mile-high plume of steam rising from Lake Michigan. The only hit in Chicago reduced a condo under construction to a rubble of part-melted steel and concrete. For the families of eight construction workers, the damage was devastating. Yet that UHO made little impact on the city's day to day functioning. What affected many more people, though miraculously no one got killed, was the UHO that took a big chip out of the I-694 bridge crossing the Mississippi. No large power stations hit. No nuclear facilities. A veterans hospital in Missouri. A tire factory in Oklahoma.

And, she thought in wonder, a little cottage in the middle of nowhere. She got out of the car, leaving the door open, the radio on, and turned, searching the sky. No smoke anywhere. What burn she smelled came only from her own disaster.

She sat in the car again, but didn't go anywhere. She wasn't sure where she should go.

The voices from the radio roved to frightened speculation. When would the attack end? Was it a cosmic storm or alien forces bent on destroying the earth? In that grim and yet somehow flippant tone typical of newscasters: "Is this indeed extra-terrestrial?" Another expert came on: "Astronomers are beginning to focus in the direction of Altair, a star in the constellation of…."

She woke with an unpleasant and familiar feeling: an unplaceable anxiety. She glanced at her watch, but since she couldn't remember what time it had been when she drifted off, she didn't know how long she'd been gone. Sitting in her car, engine off, radio on. Was she supposed to be somewhere?

"Europe braces for a wave of destruction," a man's voice said. She leaned toward the radio. What? Why? Had there been a major terrorist attack?

Then she looked up. She saw the ruins of her cottage, she understood. Then, from one moment to the next, she was lost. She had no idea what she was looking at. She scrabbled to understand: a row of pots and pans hung on a wall rising from ashes. She knew she should know, but she didn't.

Heart racing, she hit the scan button on the radio, as if somebody would answer over the air that essential question: What's happening to me? But the radio had more important things to say. "The Mona Lisa has been moved to an undisclosed location…." An age-quavering voice spoke in German, then a translator spoke over,

"In Berlin during the War…." A flat-voiced spokesman of some kind, "Law enforcement is erecting barricades…." A preacher ranted about God's wrath. A panel discussed potential catastrophes: China's Three Gorges Dam, Japan's shuttered nuclear power plant. Chernobyl. Three Mile Island.

At a familiar voice, the local news, it all flooded back to her. A broadcast out of Smithfield revealed no known hits in the area. She needed to report hers. They might find something, a clue. She rooted around in her purse for her phone, then turned the bag upside down and dumped it out on the seat beside her. Nothing but some wadded up tissues. Not even her wallet. Some day, she would look at her drivers license and wonder whose picture that was. Except her driver's license was destroyed, and they'd never issue her a new one. Her phone gone. No car keys—a surge of panic, then relief. The car keys dangled in the ignition. She attended the radio again.

The Navy installations at Norfolk had taken several small hits, all at a dining facility. Five dead. The Pentagon untouched. In Lorton, several houses destroyed. Three dead, two missing. The Park Service was investigating a possible hit at the Civil War battlefield at Manassas. Eventually she gathered that the worst hit in Virginia was the State Fair, up near Richmond.

She and Will had gone to the Fair every year, even after they moved here. The smells of hay and straw and animals and junk food. Exotic chickens with showy plumage, miniature pig races, sheepdog demonstrations. Bags of popcorn, cones of cotton candy that left stickiness on their chins and cheeks. Corn dogs and funnel cake. Artwork by school children on display. Giant pumpkins. They always left at nightfall, when the midway cranked up its lights and noise, and the smell of grease, salt, and sugar somehow grew stronger, and boys and girls crowded the walks, laughing and rowdy, stoned and drunk. She never told Will that while she too wanted to leave, she'd also yearned to stay.

The news reported a mounting death toll at the fair. Men, women, children. Probably many animals, too.

She didn't want to die. Not yet. But she couldn't resist fantasizing that she'd been napping, or at her desk writing. She would have died instantly, leaving not even recognizable remains to trouble those who came after her. Such finality both daunted and soothed.

She picked up the book from the passenger seat. *A Guide to the Bodhisattva's Way of Life*. Bodhisattva: a Buddhist term for someone who strives to achieve enlightenment in order to liberate all beings from suffering. She opened to a page, randomly.

Then, because of its odor,
Not even the foxes
Will come close to this body of mine;
For this is what will become of it.

These verses were about facing death square on. Or, the book having been written by an eighth-century monk, it was about renouncing the body. Another passage proclaimed the womb *the unclean field*. The purpose was to quell lust and attachment, but she'd never been able to accept the misogynistic overtones. Not that the monk wrote kindly of his own male body. *This putrid, dirt-filled machine.*

Don't make yourself too much at home in this world, the monk warned, not even in your own body.

The book had challenged her at every reading, every turn. Its prissy etiquette advice—*I should not sit with my legs outstretched*—collided with compassion so uncompromising, it entered the surreal: *During the eon of famine / May I myself change into food and drink.*

Its demands stirred her uncomfortably, deeply.

Thus, because he loves to pacify the pain of others,

He whose mind is attuned in this way
Would enter even the deepest hell
Just as a wild goose plunges into a lotus pool.

She'd placed the book on the car seat, in plain and frequent sight, just because it irked her. She put it there to question her courage. But that was a while ago. She'd hardly noticed it for who knew how long. Surprising it hadn't slid to the floor and under the seat. Probably because she drove so gingerly.

Recalling her relationship with the book was laborious and satisfying, though she knew she couldn't trust her process. She'd run up against herself using fantasy to cobble disparate recollections into a seamless chapter of her past. But it didn't matter in this case. She wasn't seeking a factual narrative. She was creating precisely the story she needed. Truth. Today was a good day.

She rested her head on the steering wheel. This—a good day. Her laughter came as a long, soft whine. She straightened with a sigh, picked up the book and opened it again, this time to a sticky note protruding from the pages.

May the frightened cease to be afraid
And those bound be freed;
May the powerless find power,
And may people think of benefiting one another.

There. She tossed the book back on the seat. That was the message. Her cottage, her belongings meant nothing. They meant no more now, maybe never had meant more, than a putrid body even a fox would disdain to sniff. Pots and pans, broken dishes. Old clothes. Words. Paper. Souvenirs. She started the engine, rolled down the driveway into the gathering twilight. She had to get going before she changed her mind. Before she lost her courage.

She would go to the fairgrounds and see what she could do to help. She didn't have anything material to offer, she thought as the car hummed along a two-lane highway, but she had her putrid body. Years ago, when they were still living in Richmond, she'd volunteered at a Red Cross phone bank for a couple of days after a hurricane—Gaston? Isabella? She wasn't sure she could handle phones, but the aid workers would come up with something for her. Some way to benefit others.

As darkness fell, her imaginings of blanket-draped victims and Red Cross vans handing out food gave way to visions of bright lights flashing in the dark, roller coaster screams, the smells of garbage, greasy sausage, and beer vomit mixed with burnt-sugar cotton candy and toasty popcorn, girls dressed in tight jeans and tops cut low to show cleavage, pimply boys with tattoos coiling their arms and crawling up their necks.

An oncoming car blared; she swerved back into her lane. Heart thudding, nerves jangled, she pulled over and turned off the motor.

The other car passed away into the night.

On either side of the road stretched fields of patchy snow, illuminated by a full moon. The air coming in the open window caressed her skin, warm and humid. She'd been cold lately, however high she turned the heat. Will would never have let her crank it up like that.

Will—where was he? She'd forgotten him—she'd lost him!

No. No. He was dead. He'd died so long ago. Twelve years. That she remembered. Twelve years without him.

Her sobs tapered off to let in the sound of summer insects. Not snow outside, but acres and acres of cotton ready for harvest.

She picked up a book from the floor, turned on the car's dome light, opened the book at random.

May all travelers find happiness

Everywhere they go,
And without any effort may they accomplish
Whatever they set out to do.

She put down the book, turned off the light.

She was sitting in her car, somewhere in Surry or Isle of Wight County, Virginia. She'd been on the way to help someone. She had a putrid body and a rotting brain. She didn't know how to get back home, or if she even had a home.

And all around, like magical popcorn, cotton fields glowed under the moon.

•••   •••

Petro-09

IT WASN'T HARD to let everyone think I was evil and crazy: a woman who'd killed her own baby. I figured I actually did kill him, dumping him near a landfill where a pack of wild dogs could fight over his flesh. Still, whenever a cloud of dust arose from under the feet of a stranger, I wondered if said stranger might be my son, seeking to avenge himself or just wanting to clap eyes on his long-lost mother. It was an idle habit. An idiotic habit, I should say.

The day that particular cloud of dust enveloped a stranger scootering from the Intersector pad toward the refinery, you and your bratty little gang as usual ran to mob him for candy, tokens, and whatever trinkets you could beg or steal. But as he came closer you fell back, hushed and strangely excited. I soon saw why. A dust veil hid his face.

In a sector so backward that even the Intersector pad remained unpaved, the only nonPetros we ever saw were the rare visiting trader and Security Masters venturing outside the refinery offices to snoop around town. This one wasn't Security. Despite the pretentious dust veil, he had to be only a trader. Just as my son might be, were he alive, his features a Master's but his birthmark—a reddish, shovel-shaped splotch by the right corner of his mouth—ensuring he would enjoy a low-Dom Masterhood. Just like the trader pulling up in front of my emporium.

I stood stolid as a rock on the porch, staring into the wavering heat and ignoring my heart trying to slam its way out of my chest. Hopefully his wares were of decent quality. Not too decent, though, or I wouldn't be able to sell them. On the other hand, I forced myself to muse, he could be just a worker. Someone made hideous by disease or chemicals or forge fire. Or an ex-con whose re-featurement had gone wrong, so they'd given him nice clothes and a comfy position in the refinery. About two-thirds through my time in a Granite sector, a rock slide had maimed my right foot. Everyone called it luck. The Masters clipped hard labor off my sentence and assigned me a run-down emporium on Petro-09. A chance to redeem myself, they said.

Thus I tried to quell with fruitless speculation and useless memories the hope and fear surging through my veins.

Yes, of course. You're so smart, you've already guessed that it was, indeed, my son. Why else would I bother to tell the story? You knew it right from the moment "that particular cloud of dust" rose. Meanwhile, I'm standing on my porch, fool me, still waiting to find out, arms crossed, face fixed in its "welcome to my establishment" expression. You think that makes you more clever than me.

Well, you haven't been spiked with the thought, a thousand times as a thousand clouds of dust rose from the Intersector pad: my son might be in that carrier. You haven't felt hope and fear wither on seeing other women's sons trudge through town or up the steps of my establishment.

None too soon, the trader came up my porch steps. No trudging, though. He had a light tread, the kind only Masters had. You and your buddies gawked and buzzed and hopped up and down. Even the porch flies in front of Roudo's saloon lowered their bottles to stare.

I bowed. "Welcome to Sarag's Emporium and Tearoom, Master. You're looking at Missus Sarag herself." Formerly Cynth of cool, green Clement-01, I added silently, as always.

"Ashmar, a simple trader." He took off his hat, and the veil with it.

A shovel-shaped red blotch touched the right corner of his mouth.

Joy and terror surged inside me—but I'd learned something at Granite. Thirty years of chopping rock had given me a face of stone. I showed not a glimmer of recognition or emotion.

He blinked and squinted, even on my shady porch. His skin was baby-smooth, his hair a wiry mat.

"Come in and take some refreshment, if you please, Master Ashmar." I ushered him in, discreetly turning the sign beside the entry to "closed" as I followed. You ducked in under my arm and disappeared, to touch up the tea room, I hoped.

Whenever a person entered my establishment for the first time, I reveled as they took it all in, from the pleasant swish of the fly curtain behind them, to the blended smell of abundance punctuated by machine oil, smoke, and coffee, to the fat sacks of food, to the neatly arranged shelves of cans, dishes, fabric, and whatnot. Sarag's Emporium carried all the things a household might need, plus a few useless items that people craved from the moment they set eyes on them. With shrewd dealing and the hard-earned strength of my back and arms, I'd turned a clapboard shack into a horn of plenty. I was too preoccupied for pride, though, as Ashmar duly paid his compliments.

He'd shown no more sign of recognition than I had. Seeking his mother might have brought him here.... No, seeking me was the only thing that would have brought him here. But he wouldn't recognize me. For one thing, the last and only time we'd laid eyes on each other, he'd just shoved his way out of my womb. For another thing, I'd "changed" since then.

My hair removed, my face re-featured, my name replaced, my home sector who knows how far away: Cynth of Clement-01 and Sarag of Petro-09 were truly two different women. Any motherly tenderness that might have once touched my face had been hammered off working granite. And by what I'd done.

Like any trader passing through, satchel bulging with samples and brochures boasting the tawdry goods permitted in this sector, Ashmar extolled the neatness, the bounty, the taste of my establishment. "A complete emporium, Missus," he wound up. "I can't imagine anyone in this sector would feel want."

"Thank you, Master. I do my best for the people. Excuse me a moment." I turned from him and hissed, "Sella!"

You scampered from the tea room. As ugly then as you are now, at least you'd had the sense to smooth your hair and wash your hands and face. You even remembered to curtsy to our guest. "Yes, Missus?"

"Take the Master to wash the dust from his feet and hands. Then coffee and seed cakes and the hubble-bubble. Rixi blend." This was an occasion for quality smoke. I just had to be careful not to get too stoned.

While my visitor took a piss and, hopefully, washed his hands, I plumped the cushions in what I was pretentious enough to call the tearoom: a corner scattered with some gaudy carpets, a few couches and low tables, and two palm trees. The palms were my pride and joy, though you hated them. Yes, I know. You're the one who had to haul water for them. Some caged birds made a cheerful noise.

"What beauty!" Ashmar exclaimed as you officiously led him in.

"You're too kind, Master," I said. "Please make yourself comfortable and easy."

He sat on the couch across from me, putting his satchel on the floor near his feet. You set the refreshments on the table, all pretty-pretty with doilies under the snacks and fake tortoise-shell zarfs holding pearlescent cups.

"Thank you, young girl," Ashmar said.

You simpered; I gave you the evil eye, and you backed away, your lower lip jutting.

I reflected that, had I not been forced to leave my son to the tender mercies of wild dogs or rather, as it turned out, to the Masters who found him and stole him for their own, I would have married him off by now. My grandchild would be bringing me and a distinguished guest coffee and snacks, not you, a sullen girl whose father had been bent so low by addiction, he'd sold one daughter to me and the other, prettier and more ill-fated, to the saloon-keeper. And I wouldn't be stuck in P-09. I would be home in Clement-01, drinking fine tea in my husband's house.

He'd cursed me, my husband had, when our newborn son went missing, and cursed me again when they found the midwife's body. I spent thirty years of my life breaking rocks while he went free, knowing full well he owed his rotten life to me. My only hope for justice is that he knocked up another woman less resourceful than I am.

It was a bitter train of thought I often indulged, freshly salted by the sight of my son sitting across from me, seemingly oblivious to the irony of his presence here.

We sipped and nibbled and chatted. I smiled again and again, and my mouth went dry again and again as our conversation brushed even lightly on anything connected with my past: the lack of trees in this sector compared with the Rainy sector or the Granite sector; how the beautiful rugs on the planks resembled some his father had acquired in a Clement sector. If I slapped you when you finally brought the hubble-bubble, it was only that I badly needed that smoke.

I managed not to shake as I pincered up an ember to drop in the bowl, and wondered if I would gather the courage to explain that I'd been barely more than a child, a terrified child, when I'd left him on a heap of garbage, with a moldy couch cushion for a cradle. To explain that I had no choice. The Masters executed parents of Mixed, which he'd plainly been: a baby who to all appearances was a Master, even if disfigured, dropped out of a Clement womb. Baby "Master Ashmar" would have been killed, too, or worse. The lowest Salt sectors, I'd heard, were loaded with Mixed.

And here he was, alive. My son had lived. Not only that: he lived as a Master.

Part of me longed to ask what his life had been like, how he had been found, how he had found me. The other part of me, stronger and wiser, prevailed.

If he actually did know who we were to each other, then he knew what a risky game he played. A Mixed posing as a Master, even innocently, courted a very painful execution. As for me, concealing the whole mess in the first place would earn me an equally unpleasant demise. You, girl, would have been re-sold, probably as a chippy, never mind your tender years. And with your looks, it wouldn't be in a relatively decent, and at least private, room above a saloon, like your sister. They'd have stuck you in a crib.

Don't ask, isn't a crib what you put babies in? Just don't ask, child.

My visitor from another world took a hit on the hubble-bubble, but only to be polite: he didn't hold it in. So I took a little hit, too, though I longed to fill my lungs to bursting and hold in the smoke until the room went purple.

"Have you come far, Master Ashmar?"

"Oh, yes." He pointed up. "I come from Dominion-12."

I stretched my lips in a smile as fake as my teeth. "That's very far, Master." Not that I had the slightest idea how near or far up in the sky any Dom might be.

"My father's people live there," he said.

I poured more coffee. The anger that boiled up inside me didn't flush my face or furrow my brow, or stop my mouth from babbling pleasantries about local flora and fauna, and how P-09 thrived. Nor did I share the rumor that P-09 was about played out. Not that a Master wouldn't know; he just wouldn't know that we knew.

His "father's people," of course, were not his true kin. His real father, I could have told him, was a lying bastard who never revealed that he was a born Master, under his Clement facade.

A Master who got re-featured, even just to Clement, would have to be guilty of a particularly heinous crime. So heinous, in fact, the only reason he'd been spared was the fact that they executed high Masters even more rarely than they re-featured them.

He certainly would have been sterilized, though.

After my stupefaction at seeing the midwife hold up a Master baby, after my panic, after the killing the midwife and disposing of the baby, I wondered how my husband managed to get me pregnant in the first place. One of the other women in Granite told me it happened sometimes. Vasectomies come undone.

At least he'd done me the favor of testifying that I'd been getting crazy, violently at times, as I drew near to giving birth. He claimed, too, that I'd been unfaithful. Lies, every bit of it, but the truth would have seen me executed for infanticide. Of course, his lie also happened to spare him, as he well knew. Telling the truth would have gotten both of us killed.

This lovely son of ours took another little hit on the hubble-bubble, barely breathing it in, though he let the smoke curl slowly from his nose. The one time I saw a fire snake, it had exhaled just like that....

I pulled in my wits. "And what is a lofty personage such as yourself doing in this sunburnt place?"

He touched the satchel. "I'm here to get moon rocks for trade."

The standard and only joke of this town was to sell a stranger a moon rock. I used them as douceurs for traders who didn't know that they could walk a quarter mile out of town to get a thousand more at the crater. A warehouse full of them was worth less than the dollop of honey I stirred into my coffee.

"I only hope I can get a few past the Security Master at the sector gate without paying duty," he said. "They warned me he's zealous, and they weren't joking!" A dimple touched his cheek. "But after all, I managed to smuggle myself in."

My heart drummed harder. Was it a hint? Smuggling himself, a Mixed, past Security. Just like he'd done his whole life long, actually. But he wouldn't know that. Would he? It was impossible to decide which was more improbable: that my long lost son had sought me out and found me, or that this whole encounter was an endearing little coincidence.

Or was he onto something else? Namely, my own special little "moon rock."

No. If Security had learned about that, they wouldn't bother to arrive incognito. They would simply come and seize it, and me, and all my property. Including you, runty slave girl that you were. But we were safe. No one would suspect a rundown old bitch like me of possessing a gemstone the size of my arthritic thumb.

I'd stolen it more to get back at my husband than for its beauty. Maybe I'd done him a favor instead, given that he must have stolen it himself. Now I was stuck with it. Whatever scheme I concocted to get rid of it, even just throwing it into the crater, I feared someone would report me. I could buy nothing with it, do nothing with it, except gloat over it now and then, like a fire snake mothering its hoard.

"Sella!" I called.

You popped right up, having taken it on yourself to water the palms, for once without a slap to prompt you. "Yes, missus?"

"Go sweep the porch."

You scuffled away, pouty at losing your chance to peek and eavesdrop. I listened until I heard the fly curtain and then the clamor of the other kids and your bossy little voice over them, bragging, no doubt, about having seen the trader close up. Then I excused myself to fetch some moon rocks to trade.

It took a while.

I had to think.

I had to…select.

Back in the tearoom, I settled on the couch. "Close your eyes," I said, a coy note in my voice.

He closed his eyes.

When I said he could look again, a pile of crater rocks lay before him. Plus one.

He gave a laugh, at what, I couldn't say. I observed that his teeth were white and straight and his own. He glanced toward the front door and, as I had, listened. You screeched something, mimicking me, probably, and the rest of the brats laughed. He leaned over the coffee table and took my hands in his.

The last time I'd touched those hands, they'd been tiny. Tiny. Now, trembling, they enveloped mine. Yet they felt just as childish, lacking the calluses of labor just as his face lacked the lines of care.

"Mother," he whispered.

I smothered the emotions that wanted to rise on hearing the word "mother" said to me. I yanked my hands away. "I don't know who you are, or why you picked me out for your little prank."

He opened his mouth, maybe to try again, but I cut him off.

"Let us conclude our business, Master." I didn't need to voice the threat implicit in my rudeness. We concluded our trade, and he left without another word.

Rumor had it that the trader never did pass back out of the sector gate.

Who knows? That zealous Security Officer he complained about might have discovered in him the crime of being Mixed. Or found in his satchel a stolen, thumb-sized gemstone.

I'm not sorry for what I did. I killed my son once to save his life, and I killed him again to save you, an ugly, ill-natured slave girl I'm foolish enough to consider as a daughter.

Yes, yes, and to save my own skin.

You may think you understand how things work, girl. I admit, you're clever. You know where we are. But you don't know how we got here. So stick this in your little mind. Whatever you do, the way it turns out is never what you expect.

This story isn't over yet.

01 THE HOSTLER'S STORY (FAITHFUL)

THE VID ABOVE the saloon door showed the street outside, sun-beaten and bone-white.

"All right," Ray said.

The bouncer leaned forward on his stool to clip the peace ties off his weapons. Clink! into the bucket.

Ray put the sole of his right boot to the door, painted metal scratched and scuffed from a thousand other boots. His hands rested light upon his weapon grips, but he dared not draw. Religious diversity or no, if Security caught you drawing without sufficient provocation, it was jail. He just prayed he'd be able to see if his father awaited in the blind-bright street, weapons drawn. Sufficient provocation.

He bent his leg.

Now!

He kicked open the door and jumped out, both hands tightening on his grips. Heart hammering, he squinted up and down the street.

Dad was nowhere in sight.

He breathed again, eased his hands from his weapons, adjusted his hat for no reason, and clomped down the porch steps to the plank sidewalk. Foolish precautions. Probably. When Dad gunned him down, it wouldn't be in the middle of the street. He wouldn't lay in ambush, either. Probably.

And "probably" wasn't "an acceptable level of risk," as they said at the refinery. Dad had a dead-eye and a set of weapons that could blow his son's sorry heart clear out of his chest.

Sarag's little slave girl shook a rug from the porch of the Emporium. Ray stuck out his tongue at her and she giggled and flapped the rug at him as he passed.

He hesitated in front of the Temple, then went on up the steps and through the paint-blistered door. In the vestibule, the refinery's reek of burned oil and sulfur hit him. It blanketed Petro-09, yet he never noticed it except in the Temple, as if dust and incense made it real.

You were supposed to peace-tie weapons before going in, but he didn't wake the sexton. He didn't take off his boots either, or his hat, as he slipped through the sanctuary.

He guessed their sanctuary was identical to every other Faithful sanctuary in the Dominions. A windowless room just big enough to crowd in one hundred Faithful. Painted cinderblock walls, a stand of smoky, paraffin votives, scrubbed cement floor scattered with cheap rugs and cushions to sit on. In the middle, the altar, carved of wood.

Its unstained emptiness struck him with a pang of guilt and fear as familiar as the Temple itself.

Once he brought a driver to visit. Not being one of the Faithful, the driver didn't see the altar for what it was. He said it was like the hull of a little boat. Then he had to explain what a boat is. "But with no keel," he said, "she'll go in circles." Ray didn't ask what a keel was, nor did he explain why the altar was made like a vessel.

Old Shane and Liza sat near the altar muttering mantras, beads clicking through their fingers. They were pretty much fixtures at the temple, but he was surprised to see Pru, the chippy from Roudo's saloon, sitting near the back.

At the sight of him, the corners of her mouth went down. She probably came in the Temple to get away, and in strolled one of her customers. He gave her a nod, and she shut her eyes. They were big and amber-colored. When she closed them, her face had not much left to recommend it.

As he dipped his knee to the altar, a Security Master bustled from the passage leading to the office. Given he wasn't hustling along someone in restraints, he must have breezed through to do an audit or ask some questions. He gave a little wave like they did, fingers wiggling, and kept going, even speeding up a little. Ray waited until he heard Security's craft firing up out back, then continued through to the office.

So-called, the office was no more than a lean-to furnished with a table, a couple of plastic chairs, and a plastic file box, all set on a big square of imitation-wood sheet-vinyl.

"Son, you're supposed to tie your weapons," Dad said. His own weapons hung loose in the belt slung over his chair back.

Ray sat in the orange chair. "What was Security doing here? I hope you're not in trouble." Though it would save him a world of tears or his life, if they took Dad away.

Dad smiled a little, as if he might have been thinking exactly the same thing. "Routine audit."

"Shining up his badge, I reckon. Spying around."

"Well, he didn't score any points here. Everything's tax stamped and filed in perfect order." Dad dropped the pile of ledgers into the file box. "Be right back."

Dad stepped to the sanctuary. Ray pondered how surprised the Master had looked when he saw him.

No, not surprised. Scared.

The Masters would look right through him or Dad alone, but seeing them together left no doubt they were father and son. Two of a kind, Mom used to say, born hostlers. Limber enough to reach all the tractor controls, of a size to fit comfortably in the cab.

The Masters agreed. They'd been made hostlers as soon as they came of working age. The Masters knew enough about the Faithful to put Dad and him at opposite ends of the facility. The Security Master who'd scurried through today probably feared they would exercise their religious rights in front of him, and didn't want to deal with it.

Maybe that's why Mom died so young, Ray thought. She didn't want to be around for it either. He heaved out a sigh just as his father came back in.

"What's that about?" Dad asked.

"Just thinking about Mom."

"She's in a better place. She was a good, Faithful woman."

"Amen, amen, amen."

To a Master, a Petro who worked hard and followed the rules might get bumped up a sector or two in the next life, get reborn as an Ag, or even a Clement. Moving up, life after life, until finally, he or she might attain, as they said, a Master birth.

It wasn't like that to the Faithful, though. To them, being stuck in the sectors was an affliction, whether as a Master in a Dominion palace or in the depths of a Salt sector. Death delivered the Faithful beyond sectors, beyond Dominions, beyond the sun that bleached P-09 and everything in it to the color of dirty cement.

Thus, the whispered teachings, passed on only from ear to ear.

P-09's charter permitted Religious Diversity, but technically, they were all denominations of the Masters. And while the Masters tolerated the Faithful's particular practices, outright heresy was another story.

"You've been drinking," Dad said, "and smoking."

"Drinking, not smoking. Don't need to smoke in the saloon. Breathing does it for free."

"You'll get cancer."

"I'll take a good healthy walk around the crater after my shift."

They both laughed. The effluence dump stained the lowering sun brownish red. Dad opened his own little saloon, the bottom drawer of his desk.

"Your woman visited today." He took out a bulbous blue bottle and two little clay cups. "Was she still here when you came in?"

"Pru's not my woman. But, yeah, I saw her. Did you talk to her?"

"No. I don't think she needed to talk. She just wanted sanctuary. Poor girl."

"She's a homely biscuit, for sure, but I reckon she's content enough." Ray heard and wondered at the edge in his voice.

Dad poured out shots of agave.

The drink went over Ray's tongue as earth and something like sour laundry and cucumbers, down his throat as fire, and back up to his head as a fresh, swift wind. He closed his eyes to savor the sacramental moment. He knew Dad was doing the same.

The wind died down and Dad spoke again. "Content, you say. To be a sex-worker in that place? Do you know how she ended up there?"

"She's a slave."

"That's right. Her father got kicked down from P-07 for bad debts. He racked up more debts, sold his daughters, and got shot in a drug deal. Too bad he didn't get himself shot sooner."

Dad was no liar, but Ray said, "How come I don't know about all that?"

"You tell me how come you don't know about all that."

"Were we here?"

"No, we were still on P-10. Pru was fifteen or so when she got sold to Roudo. Her little sister went to Sarag. I guess that's not too bad, even if Sarag's a tough one. Did time in a Granite sector."

Ray wasn't ready to take all this in, so he settled for the least toxic angle. "Sarag's a con?"

Dad shook his head. "We've been here three years and you don't know anything."

I'm not a priest, Ray said, but not aloud. Because if he were a priest, his father would be dead.

He shrugged. "I work all the time."

"Work. And sleep. And drink. And play cards. And do custom with Pru once a pay period. She tried to kill herself once. That made your saloonkeeper mad all right."

He's not my saloonkeeper, he wanted to say, but Dad was right. If he wasn't eating, sleeping, praying, or on shift, he hung out at the saloon.

One time he went in there to find Roudo with his fists covered in blood and the big mirror behind the bar in shards. It must have cost a months' take, and Roudo broke it and tore up his hands in a stupid rage. And everyone knew that Pru's face looked the way it did because someone's fists had worked on it. Her own father, or Roudo, or an over-amped shiftworker.

So what was he supposed to do? Change saloons? Stay downstairs at Roudo's? How would that help Pru? He was always gentlemanly towards her.

This was the reality: Pru and him, they were both shiftworkers. Her face got ruined by a beating; tomorrow or the next day his face and everything attached to it could be blown away when someone improperly tapped a carrier tank in the shipping yard.

"I guess I could learn more about her," he said. "Find out her story. But maybe she doesn't want to get into it. I don't know."

Feeble, but Dad didn't call him on it. He just gave it a chance to sink in, let his son hear it for himself, before he answered.

"It doesn't matter if you're here or in a saloon, downstairs or upstairs. You're a Faithful man. Everywhere and always."

Ray looked down at the floor. He knew what Dad was saying. But again his thoughts stayed silent inside him: I love the Faithful, but I don't want my place in it. I don't want to duel you on the dusty street between here and the saloon.

Or he could do him right here. Over many brooding sessions, he'd arrived at the conviction that Dad would prefer that. He'd rather his son came in here, stood waiting while he put on his belt and took hold of his grips. Then his son would draw his weapons and finish it. Mom had told him, Dad did it pretty much that way with his own father. But Ray was determined Dad would make the first move. Selfish, maybe, but he'd made up his mind. Ray got up, put on his hat.

Dad stood. Without looking away from his son, he put on his belt. His hands settled on his weapons grips. They faced each other square on.

Ray drew both weapons and discharged them.

Dad reeled back, his gray coveralls blooming red at his chest. Ray caught him right before he fell and pulled him into his arms. He made not a sound. The long, whining groan came from his son.

Ray wished he could go back in time ten, twenty seconds. An hour. A day. A year.

A life.

Dad's head fell forward and his blood poured out of his mouth hot onto his son's shoulder. His hands slid from his son's back and dangled at his sides, and still Ray held him tight, held him up against himself. Maybe he was trying to hold in his father's blood. He sobbed but didn't know if tears came out.

Shane and Liza must have run in at the discharge. They gently pulled Dad away, and Ray stopped sobbing like someone hit a switch. Shane put his arms under Dad's arms; Liza took his feet. At a nod from Liza, they picked him up.

Ray began to follow them, then turned back to fetch his weapons. On his hands and knees in a pool of blood, he found them under the table. He stood again, his hand on the back of the chair to steady himself.

When he came in the sanctuary, they'd already laid Dad out in the altar. Liza saw the son and backed away, her head bowed. Shane wasn't there. He must have run to spread the word among the Faithful.

Today's the day, he would tell whoever was off shift.

Ray knelt at the altar. Shells weighed down Dad's eyelids, and his mouth gaped open, full of blood. A blanket covered his destroyed chest. Ray felt sick. The smell or the sight or knowing what he'd done. He stuck his hands in the altar, under Dad's neck. The blood went up just past his fingernails.

He wished he'd been born a girl—but then he saw Pru standing pressed against the wall, her eyes wide. If he were a girl, he could have ended up like that. No, Faithful don't traffic flesh. Except he did. Buying Pru's.

He went up to her but didn't touch her with his bloody hands. "Get me some clean coveralls, Pru, would you, please."

She picked up her purse from the floor beside her.

"Hey, Pru."

She looked at him, all amber eyes.

"Not if it gets you in trouble. Someone else can do it."

"I'll do it. I'm off tonight."

The Faithful came in bunches. Through the propped open door, the sky blazed sunset orange and red. He stared at it until someone took his right arm, and another his left. They guided him back through the crowd to the middle of the sanctuary and eased him down to kneel again at the altar. The sexton fanned away the flies.

The temple filled. His people now. All told, one hundred or less. Never more. The Masters permitted one hundred Faithful, max, per sector.

Such thoughts went through his mind, but crushing them down was the reality that he would never look in his Dad's eyes again, never hear his quiet, wry voice. His coveralls were soaked in blood. His mind spun, that he made this come to pass. He gripped the rim of the altar and stared down at the carpet. Dad floated in his peripheral vision. Someone cleaned his hands and arms and face and neck with wet towels.

Dad had surely known what would happen this day. The books, making sure everything was clean, putting them away so they wouldn't get messed up. He'd wanted it to be finished. He didn't want to be the one kneeling at an altar filled knuckle deep in blood.

As a Faithful son, the truth settled in Ray's heart: this was how it had to be.

As a son, that same sure heart was stove in with grief and guilt.

As a Petro, he stood up as the shift warning blared outside.

Pru waited in the passage to the office, folded up coveralls and a couple of towels in her arms. He changed in the office. Someone had mopped up most of the blood.

He had to roll the legs and sleeves of the coverall. Three amps nestled in the front breast pocket. Pru must have put them there. She didn't know that Faithful don't take them, but she did know he'd wasted most of his sleep shift at the saloon.

He left out the back door. He didn't want to go through the sanctuary, with Dad lying dead in the altar and the people looking up to him for doing the deed, even as they mourned.

His eyes stung and watered as he walked up Main Street. Not tears. A breeze drove the lingering effluence down on the town. One of the stacks flared like a giant candle. It was the same every night, but he decided to think of it as a votive for his father.

None of his crewmates were Faithful, and no one said anything, but he could tell word was out. Some of them didn't speak to him at all, their silence hard and angry. Others acted sympathetic or pitying, or nervous, or awkward, or just jaded. His partner wouldn't look him in the face, though the man had known full well what was coming and never tried to talk him out of it. The older guys kept an eye on him, watching that he didn't make a mistake that could get everyone killed. They all got through the shift.

While punching out, he glimpsed the Security Master that visited his father that afternoon. At least, he thought it was him. They looked pretty much the same to him. Soft and babyish. He imagined that all Petros looked alike to them.

Pru was waiting at the gate. "What're you doing here?" he asked.

She didn't answer, just held up his coveralls, laundered.

Away from the floodlights some stars showed. They walked to the crater. He didn't feel like going to the dorm, and she must not have wanted to go back to the saloon either, though on her night off she'd have a room to herself.

Some kids were partying around a bonfire, and people embraced here and there under blankets. They climbed up on a big, flat rock, checking it for snakes before they settled down. Pru fired up a joint, and they passed it back and forth.

Halfway down, she said, "I wish I'd had the guts to kill my father." Except with her missing front teeth, it came out, "I with I'd had the gut-th."

He toyed with his roach clip. His father had made it from a scrap of copper wire, the handle a spiral decorated with a couple of beads. He fastened the joint to it. "It wasn't like that." He didn't feel angry at her, though he could have been.

"I know. It'th juth not fair."

He thought of what his father said to him: *You're a Faithful man. Everywhere an*d always.

It hit him: those were Dad's last words to him. The grief pressing from inside seemed to throb and Ray's breath came short, even as he marveled at Dad's wisdom, not just in the words, but in the timing of them. The provocation of them, maybe. Those words and Dad's blood sealed his son as Faithful. *Everywhere and always.* He took another toke and let it out slow.

"While I killed Dad," he said, "that Master who dropped in at the temple today probably sat down at a linen-covered table to drink fine wine and eat a steak."

Pru guessed the direction of his thoughts, though she didn't quite get it right. "Killing a Mathter won't even thingth out."

"I'm not planning to kill a Master," he said. "I don't want to kill anyone ever again."

"Good."

"I want to free you," he said.

"Ha. You're not the firtht man to thay that to me. And I bet—"

"I'll be the last to say it," he broke in. His voice was harsh, but he didn't mean it toward her. "I'm going to free you, Pru. And your sister."

"Leave my thisthter be. Thee's better off with Tharag than anywhere elth in thith fucking thector."

She waved off his offer for the last hit. He took it, then unclipped the nub and tossed it off the rock.

He'd never seen any sectors but P-10 and P-09. Still, given the difference between just one degree, Pru and her sister and dad had come down quite a ways, from a 07 to a 09.

He picked up the coveralls she'd brought. They were damp. "You washed them?"

"A man from your temple helped."

"Thanks." He stood up and took off the borrowed coveralls, shook his out, then sat down again. "I'll just sit like this, if you don't mind."

"It'th not ath if I've never theen you naked before."

They both laughed. Then his thoughts sobered him up again. He lay back and closed his eyes and fell into something like a doze.

When Pru stroked him on the stomach, he was all awake in an instant. She'd already taken off her dress and underwear. Up on the rock, no one could see them. She lay down beside him and they embraced. Like never before, she let him kiss her on the mouth. After some of that, she let him put his hand between her legs. He'd never done that before, either, but she showed him what to do. She sighed and, oh, how she liked it and so did he.

The good rock took their liquids. They lay side by side holding hands on its hard back.

As his heartbeat returned to normal, he found himself thinking, he didn't see her put in her birth control. She probably did, while he was passed out, but he pretended to himself that she hadn't.

Maybe she'd have a girl, a daughter mixing his mother and herself, Faithful and kind and strong.

Or she'd have a boy, and his father would show him how to live and die Faithful, just like Dad had showed him and the rest of the Faithful.

Coming down from the weed, back to reality, he wasn't sure what to do in terms of paying. Maybe she'd given it to him for comfort, and it could hurt her feelings if he paid. Or she might be insulted if he didn't.

He didn't need to ask.

"Free," she said.

"Free," he said.

They held each other with all their might, the rock strong beneath them.

02 GARBAGE GAL'S STORY (FLING)

GARBAGE WORKERS SURVIVED eleven months, tops. But not her. She'd been flinging waste into the sun for two years. Surely neither Justice nor Security appreciated such uppity defiance of the odds. Still, she kept flinging. Law forbade interfering with cons serving out their sentences, and the Masters were, if nothing else, law-abiding.

She wasn't, quite. Three months after being sealed in, she'd found a vid device wedged between her bunk mattress and a bulkhead. One of the mechanics must have left it by accident, or for pity's sake. A square screen about the size of her two hands side by side.

A couple of cameras hidden somewhere on the shell of the garbage tug broadcast to the vid her only view outside.

The Masters would have destroyed the vid, had they known about it. Her sentence precluded such mercies. Or maybe they did know about it. They might be surveilling her, for some reason. Still, she'd jauntily mounted the vid on the dashboard. Let them watch! Bore themselves to tears.

The east loading dock of Petro-09 appeared on the screen as a silvery shine the size of her fingernail, growing on approach into a concrete slab about the size of a baseball field. Baseball! Those were the days.

As the tug entered its slot in the yard, dust and more dust obscured the vid. It settled, slowly, to reveal the shipping bay. A swarm of lumpers loaded the last waste caskets into the scow. She zoomed the screen and caught the usual jabber. No audio, but as a driver, she'd learned to lip read. You had to know what people were saying in noisy environments. It wasn't all complimentary—some of the waste caskets apparently stank to high Dominions—but she didn't mind. She liked P-09's shipping crew.

The lumpers clambered over the scow, checking the hatches, shouting through their routine "Hatch 1!" "Hatch 1 secure!" and so on and so forth. The hostler's tractor idled in the yard. A sutler scootered out with food and other supplies for the tug.

Nothing seemed amiss. Not that you could tell by watching faces, reading lips. Lumpers and hostlers would be the last to know if Security rigged a trash casket to detonate. And say one of them did suspect something, and signaled danger—not to a sealed-in garbage woman, but to their pals—with a pursed mouth or the wiggle of an eyebrow. It wouldn't help her a bit, unless you considered it a shortening of her sentence.

Encapsulated for life, no escape. Her world a cockpit, a bunk bed, a lav, a food dispenser, and curving plastic walls.

And the view from the vid.

Flinging garbage containers into the sun without flinging the tug after it took a certain knack, a certain flair. But sloppy flings might not have been what propelled her defunct colleagues into the sun along with the garbage. Maybe they flung themselves. With no vid, the only view would be those curving plastic walls.

Thumps and rumbles indicated supplies entering the closet. The sutler risked his fingers to grab a few candy bars from the chute. He slipped them in his coverall pockets.

"I saw that," she said. "Little bastard." Not that he could hear her. And not that she cared. The food was stale but plentiful, and better than what any worker got on Petro-09, or any sector, probably. Scraps from the Masters' tables.

The sutler backed off. As he trundled back to the bay, the

hostler's tractor glided forward to grab the scow from the dock and gently, as it seemed to her, maneuver it toward the tug.

"Careful now," she said. "One tap in the wrong spot will blow this refinery clear up to Dom 01."

She trusted this hostler, though. He coupled scow and tug with the grace of a dancer—the dancers back home, not the clowns who cut a caper now and then on the loading dock. Even on the night he killed his father—as she'd gathered from dock gossip—he'd been focused and productive.

That was some night. Lips moving, yacking something fierce about the killing, then stiff straight lines the second he came out on the dock. He'd been focused on work all right, but besides lips she could read faces. His rigid mouth and eyes said he was in shock.

Well, yeah, he'd blown his dad away!

She didn't begrudge the man his freedom. His chums probably got it right, saying he'd had no choice. It was just kind of funny. One of the little oddities of life. Masters let them get away with murder, but if the Masters knew what the Faithful really believed, they'd bundle the whole lot of them down to Salt, no questions asked. An old driver had told her, all hush-hush, that for the Faithful the only true freedom lay outside Dominions and sectors. In other words, the Faithful believed that the Dominion scheme was all wrong.

High heresy. Workers could kill each other in the name of Religious Diversity, but putting down the Dominions was capital heresy.

"No offense, man," she said. "We all know religions are weird."

His head moved up and down a fraction.

"You agree, huh?"

A flicker of his eye. A wink? And his lips moved.

Fling.

Her hands went clammy and her heart began pounding.

No way. He couldn't see her, hear her. For all he knew, the tug could be operated by a robot.

Fling, he'd mouthed.

"You're not cruising an old garbage bird like me?" Her chuckle this time was forced.

But his vehicle had backed out of the vid's sight line.

"Imagination of mine, don't you run me down the road to crazy." She shook her head. "As if I'm not half there already." She meant it, but she also said it in case the vid really was a Security portal. Dom forbid she got the hostler busted.

A light shudder indicated hitches engaged. The hostler headed toward the dock—

A series of numbers interrupted her view.

"What under the Doms—?" She cut herself off just in time.

The numbers vanished. The lumpers on the dock, back on-vid, speculated what it would be like to "do it" with a garbage worker. Better hold your nose! And so on and so forth. Same old dumb jokes. Little did they know that inside the tug sat a grizzled, gnarly semi-old lady. They didn't even know her gender. Sometimes their fetid fantasies made her a woman, sometimes a man, sometimes a very knowing robot. Sometimes in her bunk, she embraced their more graphic jibes.

She returned their banter with her own lame crap, but she wasn't really paying attention. The numbers from the vid glowed in her mind brighter than the numbers flickering over her console.

Point five sheltiens. Eight sheltiens. Four sheltiens....

The tug, with scow locked on, rolled slowly from the yard.

She was pretty sure the numbers were either a navigation code or a conditions code, though none she knew. Too bad she couldn't punch them in, see what happened. But the console wouldn't respond. Everything was programmed, except the fling. That's when she took over. The Masters giving garbage workers a chance to end it all. Well, to be fair, things got jumpy at the fling. Unpredictable. She called it weather with no weather reports. Her gut, not to mention thirty-some years as a driver, told her what numbers to enter.

The vid screen filled with a lift-off cloud of brown glittering dust. She repeated the sequence again and again, silently, without daring even move her lips to it.

As Petro-09 dropped away, the sky's blue deepened to indigo. "Good old Indigo," she murmured, a routine comment, though Indigo was anything but good. The only reason Indigo-11 evoked nostalgia was because it had been one of her runs in the old days. She'd pitied the workers there almost as much as she did Salts.

When the vid showed only black void and points of light, she covered it with a food wrapper. She didn't feel like looking at space.

She switched her chair's mode to WALK. "Let's take a nice stroll. Clear the mind, aid digestion." And she needed something to do, something to keep her face from showing what she'd worked out.

Impossible, but true: the vid had flashed a Doppler sequence.

The Masters held their holy of holies tighter than a tick to a dog. The only reason she recognized one, or knew of them at all, was the same reason she was a garbage gal. She'd stumbled across a Master's pad, on a Dom loading dock, and rather than pretend she'd never seen it, she'd been dumb enough to check it out. They must have been desperate for garbage workers, or they would have executed her for treason. Instead, they took her down for blasphemy and sealed her in a garbage tug.

Sealed, but not as tight as they thought. The vid. The hostler. Maybe.

And the numbers!

She'd learned from that cursed Master's pad that Doppler sequences supported every off-sector transport under the Doms. Yet as a driver, she'd never entered a Doppler sequence. Never had a clue they existed. Never even bothered, for that matter, to wonder how she and her rig got from point A to point B. A driver's job, basically, was to regulate the cargo climate, do supply and mechanical checks, and keep the log and manifests.

Sounded boring, but hands down, driving made the best job under the Doms. Maybe on the Doms, too. No other workers had such freedom. She'd toured facilities, temples and towns in five sectors, though until this gig she'd never done a Petro. Not that she was really "doing" P-09. Being a Garbage, she couldn't go out like she used to do.

And in her sealed cab, she'd never run into a hint of … whatever this was.

Treason?

Or something more than treason.

"Three cycles before we hit the fling." Three sleep-wake cycles to figure this out.

Every transport, from garbage rigs to Masters' jets to supply runs, depended on Doppler sequences. She'd learned that from the fateful pad.

"The sectors revolve around the Dominions, which sustain the workers," she droned piously. "Without the benevolence of the Masters, the workers perish."

So official cosmology had it. But this gnarly, blasphemy-spouting tug-driver says it ain't so.

More like the other way around. Workers were the ones squeezing oil from rocks, quarrying stone, chipping out salt in the dark, and paddling vats of indigo till their bones turned blue. And supplies went in both directions.

If the Doms were severed from the sectors….

They'd wink out. And what about the sectors?

The workers at Petro-09 didn't know they'd drained just about all the oil there was, in their sector. The Masters did, and they were ready to deal with it. Not far outside P-09's border was a vast tract of land laid out neat as a Security Master's uniform with fields, sheds, housing, barns, seed stores, livestock pods, irrigation. All they needed to do was drop in workers—after, presumably, transferring the P-09s to another Petro sector—and an Ag sector would go live.

The Petros had no idea it was even there. All they knew of their world was the refinery's smoggy, metallic sprawl and, stretching away from it, a jumble of dirt streets and frame buildings with tin roofs: dorms, a couple of saloons and cafes, temples, the jail, supply stores, machine shops, training schools—the concerns of a refinery workforce.

No wells, no cisterns. Even with the community reservoir replenished weekly, water was scarce. No one could keep a garden, let alone livestock. They didn't need to. With everything delivered, no one bothered to do anything but work, party and/or pray, and sleep.

"What would we do without supply runs and Masters' plans?"

Just the thought of a sector going without supply runs made her stomach twist. Yet she couldn't let it go.

She slowed the chair's pace to a stroll. "No use working up a sweat. It's not like we're in a hurry to get anywhere."

She could be way wrong. The numbers could merely *seem* like a Doppler sequence. Her imagination making up a fake DS. Not close enough to fool a Master, but close enough to fool someone like herself. Not that many like herself existed.

Or maybe a lot of workers did know about the Doppler sequences. Like the hostler who mouthed "fling." And the mechanic who left the vid in the tug. And whoever set up the numbers in the vid. And made them appear right after the hostler said his line. And who knew who else. Maybe even the Master who left his pad unattended on a loading dock for a driver to find.

Nah. No way.

But.

Say the numbers were a Doppler sequence, and someone had planted this vid in this tug because they knew, or at least hoped, this driver would find it. Then what?

She uncovered the vid. "Let's look at space a while. Maybe we'll catch a comet."

She dozed, and dreamed of scow and tug touching—and woke up in the "night" with a gasp.

The fling and the Doppler sequence.

It came together in her mind, the pieces touching as gently as the scow kissing the tug—as lightly as a tractor mis-tapping a refinery tank.

An explosion, or something like that.

"No!" She stopped herself from dashing the vid off the console. "Stop being crazy. Where do you get these ideas anyway?"

And hush up!

"No comet's gonna hit you," she said for whoever might be surveilling the vid.

A sleep-wake cycle's worth of desperate distraction failed to dislodge the equation.

Fling plus Doppler sequence.

Equals.

An explosion.

Or something like that.

Word puzzles, number games, memory-building a whole city out of places she'd been—nothing took her mind off of it.

"Okay, I give up." She punched a veggie cocktail from the food machine. "Let's play it out."

The straw broke off—most of her food was sound, but often had packaging defects. "Still drinkable."

Let's say a conspirator put the vid in here, just so an old garbage gal can see a hostler say some crap about having a fling. Then, coincidentally, a DS pops up on the vid.

She sipped the cocktail. "Pretty tasty."

DS on the vid plus hostler mouthing fling equals....

What?

"A bit of celery, tomato juice, and who knows what else. Beetles and eels for all I know."

Not just any fling. The next fling. Because the hostler never said anything until now. And what's the Faithful slogan? *Today's the day.* So, next fling, we enter the Doppler sequence in the controls.

Then what?

"Unfortunately, no liquor."

Or maybe the real question is, has said old garbage gal finally gone completely nuts?

"Some cocktail."

No.

Mistaken, maybe. Not crazy. She'd been careful about that.

She wadded up the cocktail cup and, though she wasn't hungry, popped it in her mouth.

She could play a mind game. Imagine all this was by design of the Masters, from her finding the Master's pad to the hostler mouthing "fling." To use a Doppler-type term, that just didn't resonate.

So, pretend she was on the right track. Pretend that entering the DS at the fling would take down a transport grid. What was the point?

For herself personally, revenge. Revenge for what they'd done to her. Taken her away from her life, from everyone she loved and everyone who loved her. She'd tried not to think on that too much. Just another road to crazy.

But taking down a grid would kill workers, too, not just Masters. It would be mass murder.

Or mass salvation.

Their supply lines severed, the Masters would have nothing to sustain them. But the workers, or at least some of them, could save themselves. They could wander to that Ag area. Work it. Eat their own harvest.

They could live. If they survived. But whatever happened to everyone else, one thing was certain.

This old garbage lady will go bye-bye. Because you can't fool around with a fling.

She gave a grunt of laughter.

You can't change the cosmos and keep your tug from hurling into the fiery sun at the same time.

She'd die without ever living again.

At the trial, she'd imagined they would find her innocent. After the verdict—*you've made a big mistake!*—and after she was sealed, she'd come up with a plan to prove herself innocent of treasonous intent. She would do her job cheerfully and well. If the vid was a surveillance device, all the better.

She'd pretended to the vid, elaborately, that she didn't understand what she'd seen, on the Master's pad, about Doppler sequences and how the transport grids depended on them. *I just don't understand Master stuff. But I guess that's why they're Masters and I'm a worker.* Like she had no idea that a handful of numbers kept the Dominions going. *I can barely remember navigation sequences.* She'd pretended that it never occurred to her, the Masters lived by those numbers and whatnot.

Holy of holies and whatnot.

Sometimes keeping it in made her feel like she'd bust. Still, she'd never said it aloud: Doppler. Unfortunately, of course, she had. After the Master caught her with his pad and before she had a chance to think it through.

The fantasy of freedom persisted despite reality.

"Ain't that the point?"

If she acted dumb, they could see for themselves how harmless she was.

To be in a saloon again, drinking and smoking with her buddies, cheating at cards, throwing insults, cracking nasty jokes. Then jumping in a bunk with one of them all drunk and dirty for some low-down fun. Next morning, oh the moaning and groaning, oh the hangover. *Take a powder, ya silly bitch!* Then dash to the dock for the next run, and more of the same on the other end. A few lucky times she'd crossed runs with her mother, a driver herself, and the two of them had kicked up the shit with a rare old binge.

She could drive herself bonkers, daydreaming of the old life.

Mom had been away on a run during the trial. Didn't get to see her girly one last time. None of her buddies there to wave goodbye, either. The Masters made sure of that. No one had seen her off.

Revenge sure was a tempting notion.

DS on the vid plus hostler mouthing fling equals nothing. Or equals a downed grid and a Dom cut off.

Equals lots of Masters dead as fish on a nice, sandy, Clement river bank. With the sun beating down on them.

But—equals lots of workers dead?

And/or—equals lots of workers free?

In addition to some mighty weird tenets, like the priest's son killing his dad or vice versa, the Faithful held that life and not-life—things like stones and sand and sky and water—connected to each other like gears, like parts of a machine. When one thing turned, the next thing turned, and the next thing and the next, and on and on. That was how the cosmos came to be and how it kept going. Each little thing took part in churning it all out.

To the Faithful, this scheme was both good and bad. It was love, they said, but it was the opposite of free.

"That's what I don't get."

She laughed, a sincere laugh, not just for the vid. "Getting deep here. Not a job for simple minds."

The job for this simple mind was to decide what she would do, a half sleep cycle from now, when she hit the fling.

Equals, without a doubt, one dead garbage woman.

It didn't matter if the whole plot was a figment of her imagination, or if it really was a plot. Or whether said plot succeeded or failed. If her hands didn't enter normal, proper navigation numbers at the fling, she would burn.

She'd seen a lift driver engulfed in flames when his vehicle pulled a spark. Saw him jerk and writhe, heard the screams. Could still hear the screams. She'd wondered, much later, if he'd been a con set up to serve as a safety warning.

Revenge, yeah, but against herself as much as anyone else. Not only would she die, she'd die very painfully.

How did that fit into the Faithful's ever-loving cosmic machine?

They claimed that freedom lay beyond Dominions and sectors. It didn't matter whether you worked your way up or got kicked down. You had to break free once and for all. No more Masters, no more workers. No… nothing?

She stared at the vid. Stared into space.

There had to be more to it than that. The Garbage Gal smiled.

Love couldn't just be the opposite of freedom.

03 EXILE'S STORY (TO TOUCH THE EARTH, TO FEEL THE SUN)

UNLIKE OTHER EXILES—UNLIKE her husband—the Exile had not been forced down to a lower sector. Not forced, like him, from slavery in an oil refinery to slavery in a salt mine. On the contrary. She had risen up, up, up, all the way up to a Dominion, and not as a servant but as a Master. Low-ranked, to be sure, a mere Flight Master, but still, a Master.

Her "ascent," to use the term from the Book of Dominions, was not a posthumous reward for being a docile worker. With the help of other conspirators, she'd evaded capture, then cheated her way up.

Her confederates re-gendered her, re-featured her. They trained her to walk and talk as a Master and as a man, and to play the role of a Flight Master who had neither the ambition nor the family influence to advance beyond piloting small, inter-Dominion carriers. And a real sober-sides, her colleagues scoffed, never without the Book in hand. No one knew that each time she opened it, she spit in it. They soon gave up inviting her to carouse.

Her beloved died within two years, as Salt convicts generally did.

In exile from her body and her home, she lived two lives, one outside, one inside—outside as a male Flight Master, inside as a Petro woman.

In the carrier's cockpit, for example… Her manly fingers pranced over the console, running routine frequency tests; her rough voice barked commands to the driver. But her mind, her spirit dwelled in a turquoise blue sky soaring over redrock carved and curved by wind and rain. A jaunty bird sassed the world from a juniper shrub studded with silvery-blue berries—

"These overnights are a bore." Milden's voice carried from the adjoining Master cabin. The husband of the elderly couple sharing the cabin answered, but too quietly for Exile to make out his words.

Exile switched her monitor to porthole. The workers didn't have access to any monitors. If they did, if they could see space, would they have found its vast sameness ugly, disconcerting? She had, at first, but eventually made herself find loveliness and even poetry in the bottomless black with its glittering spill of stars.

She had forced herself to accept that she would never again stand under a starry night sky grounded and graced by an earth. The carriers she piloted served Dominions, where her shoes touched only metal or plastic, where everything not manufactured was contrived: plants grown hydroponically and animals bred for ornament or consumption. Her sunlit skies, her redrock and junipers and the clever, quick creatures that lived among them—all fantasy. Her past, a fantasy. She hadn't walked on dirt for years. Her colleagues who had to travel to earths made a show of envying her.

She watched the Master cabin monitor as Milden plucked at the front of his tunic and shifted his buttocks in the gently heated seat. She couldn't shake the feeling that he was Security. The seat vids stocked the latest entertainments, but from what she could see he flicked only through the channels that spied on the worker cabin.

In there, on benches along the walls, sat two young men, a young woman, a mother and father and their little girl, and a middle-aged man. A serving man polished drinking glasses at the canteen. All wore brown coveralls, but the child's had ruffles sewn on at wrists and ankles. Shiny shoes—so tiny!—peeked out from under the drab flight blanket her mother had tucked around her. Her parents were bringing her to a better life: service on a mediocre resort Dominion.

Exile began a series of routine checks. Paused. Started again, as if her heart had not just about stopped, and was now thudding so hard, her ears throbbed.

The passenger manifest for the worker cabin listed two young men—Reed and Blu. And a young woman named as Tyny.

Tyny Blu Reed.

Exile's articles of faith lay not in the Book of Dominions, but in the certainty that the minuscule threads she had manipulated slowly and carefully over years would weave together with those her husband and others had manipulated, also slowly and carefully over years. When it all converged, so would her divergent lives, Exile and Petro woman, culminating with the destruction of the Doppler Bridge.

Some day.

The day that *small colorful flutes* appeared on the manifest of whatever inter-Dom carrier she happened to be piloting.

Tyny Blu Reed. Small colorful flutes.

Today.

She had begun every trip, from her first as a Flight Master to this one, with the silent mantra: *Today is the day.* She'd made it part of her preflight routine, along with the minuscule alterations she made to each carrier she piloted. Familiarity equals readiness, as they taught in flight school. Even when the cargo manifest didn't list a crate of painted piccolos or pied recorders, even when she knew she would normalize the carrier post-flight, she made the preflight alterations.

She had recited it to herself, hundreds of times: *Today is* the day. *Today is* the day.

She evened her breath and kept her face fixed, she hoped, in the expression of a jaded, but competent Flight Master.

"All well, driver?" Her voice scratched gruff, masculinized, its vocal patterns rearranged.

The driver answered with a routine grunt, quickly amended to, "All well, Flight Master." He was new at his job, a worker not used to working one on one with a Master.

With legs steadier than she'd hoped, she went into the Master cabin. Its padded seats formed a collegial circle, as if several unrelated Masters might find themselves striking up a conversation. Ironically, though, Masters were more paranoid than workers, and rarely socialized spontaneously.

She offered courteous, conventional greetings to the elder couple and Milden as she took a seat. The passenger manifest listed Milden's occupation as Transportation, his purpose as vacation. If he was really Security, why travel incognito on a little carrier bearing a handful of workers and a retired Master and his wife to a middling resort? They made an insignificant lot.

She put her vid on a game show but kept the sound low on her earbud. Through the opening to the cabin, she could see the servant juicing a citrus fruit.

"I don't travel this line frequently," Milden said, as if anyone cared, "but supposedly they've refurbished the casino…."

He and the Elder Master engaged in a conversation on the merits of various baccarat dealers, swimming pools, buffets. Exile strained to hear the hum that signaled the carrier's approach to the Bridge.

The Bridge. Not a physical structure, it could not be guarded, yet it was the most guarded thing under the Dominions. There was nothing of it to be destroyed, yet for ten years and more, she and a web of other conspirators had plotted to bring it down.

"Still, can't complain, I suppose," Milden said.

Since he was looking at her, she managed to return, "We're very fortunate."

She had lost the thread of the conversation. Her ears rang chronically, an irksome soundtrack, but not enough to cause deafness. Now, though, arbitrary moments of silence chopped up the routine hum and clatter of the carrier. Everything normal, then silence, then normal sound again.

He pointed his chin toward the worker cabin as he took a sip of the fresh-squeezed juice. "So are they."

She nodded. "So they are."

He might have meant, they were lucky to be going to casino jobs, or he might have meant lucky to be traveling in this carrier. True enough, normally. In most carriers, workers sat on metal benches so close together that rows of knees bumped rows of buttocks. The air hung rank and heavy, and sustenance came in the form of nutri-chunks and cleansed urine. Entertainment, for the workers and for the Masters watching on vids, took the form of story-telling and fights, which presented some interesting logistics in crowded quarters, as did getting to the toilets.

In small carriers such as this, worker cabins didn't provide nearly as much amusement, a fact that no doubt compounded Milden's boredom. Good: fewer worker lives would be lost when the Bridge fell. If it fell today.

Her scruples hardly mattered. The Bridge's destruction would sever Dominions and earths from each other; the infinitude of space would defeat any attempts at reunion. Life on the Dominions would be extinguished. Many people on the earths would perish, too.

But those who survived would be free.

She raised her eyes from the vid and looked at her fellow Masters with the correct degree of deference due their ranks, with a light pause on Milden to catch his eye. She let her brow wrinkle; she let a little something slip into her eyes: an inauspicious something troubled her.

"Master Milden, if I might ask, are you feeling well?"

"I feel fine." He looked genuinely surprised, but his hand went straight to the chest of his tunic. Possibly he had a medical device in there. Probably not.

She shifted her facial concern slightly toward alarm, then bowed her head. "I beg your pardon. I am forgetting the inevitable strain that travel puts on all of us." She beckoned the servant. He bowed into the cabin.

"Yes, Master?"

"Refill the iced water and bring hand towels."

"Yes, Master." He bowed out.

Years in this role had not immunized her to self-disgust at taking a high-handed manner to servants. In fact, had it been just herself and the old couple in the cabin, she might have been less peremptory.

Funny, to worry about such things when everyone in the carrier would be killed, Masters and workers alike, if the plan succeeded.

Laying it had been mind-bogglingly complex. The final step would be stunningly simple.

The carrier generated the frequency pattern by which it "caught a line" of the Doppler Bridge. Sound from inside the carrier, of course, normally had no effect.

She'd altered this carrier, however, to receive a very special tune composed over years by a conspirator. The "song" was not the refined entertainment valued on Dominions, nor an earthy worker song. It comprised, rather, a series of precise, shrill glissandos aimed at rupturing the frequency pattern.

The Exile's wrecked vocal cords hadn't nearly the precision and range required to execute the plan. Her three conspirators—small colorful flutes—would sing it. Three, in case one or two got disabled. One voice alone could sound the warbling tune that would send the carrier through the Bridge like a stone thrown through a spider's web.

Long time since she'd seen a stone or a spider's web.

The servant slipped back in with a pitcher and soft, immaculate white towels. As he arranged them on the counter, he checked the room with a technique she knew well: scan for anything out of order while avoiding eye contact with the Masters. It was a mutual game, another transaction that still came to her with effort: pretending not to see the servants. Yet they truly did not want to be seen by Masters.

Milden, however, watched the servant with great interest, interspersing glances at the Exile. He would be wondering why the Flight Master had requested towels and cold water, connecting it with himself: the area in the center of his chest, to be exact.

She gave him a slightly embarrassed smile. "Just to have on

hand." She paused, then added with patent tact, "The cabins can feel … close."

It didn't matter if he thought something in fact might be wrong with him, or if he thought her a fool. The message got through: she'd noticed him touching his chest and maybe something was wrong there.

He stopped touching his chest. She stopped suffering patches of deafness.

On an entertainment channel of her vid, a low-ranked Master clapped his hands to celebrate winning bonus servant hours for his apartment. She watched as if bored, nothing better to do, her face smooth, her emotions turbulent.

Milden's chest device canceled noise. That could only mean, it must mean, that this was the day. And Security knew it, or suspected it.

The "small colorful flutes" had been recruited and trained with infinite caution, the tune revealed to each, bit by bit, as fragments embedded in pop songs, commercial jingles, hymns. For these reasons alone, the circumstances could not be replicated.

Nor could she. The risk, the expense, the logistics of her transformation had been stupendous. The few others who underwent the procedure perished in the ordeal. The scientist who performed it had thoroughly destroyed himself and everything and everyone connected with the project, when it looked as if Security might close in. Everyone except her husband, who'd volunteered to play decoy.

As a Flight Master, she manipulated carrier schedules all over the Dominions. Her nudges to processes well-refined and jealously guarded had to be most dainty to avoid detection. She'd spent entire nights hacking one minute from a flight here, sending one servant there. She'd made subtle but potentially devastating alterations to each carrier she piloted. Just in case *Today is the day.* Except for her husband, she'd never seen the face or heard the name of another conspirator. She did know, however, that only a freak like her had both access and motivation.

Repeated surgeries and chemical infusions had acquainted her with the utmost extremes of pain, from the removal of her internal and external generative organs, to the mutation of identifiable features from her fingertips and toetips to her vocal and eye-movement patterns. She would endure it all again, rather than fail.

Her final job, at least, was straightforward. Keep the carrier on course—or rather, send it off course. And head off obstacles. Like Milden. And maybe the driver. And maybe everyone else.

She glanced at Milden now and then with a solicitous air. She sensed—hoped—that he waxed over-confident. He would let the plan begin, so he could flush out everyone involved. Meanwhile, he gazed at the vid as if unconcerned by her concern.

He might have been wondering why the Flight Master kept looking at him like that. Was his baffling device toxic, broken? His rivals would stop at nothing to best him. He turned away from the vid.

"So you're angling to be a physician?" he asked with a bland smile.

She covered her desperate amusement at his transparency with a modest chuckle. "Oh, no. Well, I used to work in my father's practice. He was a physician. But I could never pass the entrance exams. I'm doomed to be a mere flight technician." It was precisely the kind of answer that would deepen his paranoia. Utterly disingenuous. "Of course we do have some medical training, for emergencies and so forth. Once I had to—"

"What do you think is wrong with me?"

Such a direct approach, while unexpected, didn't confuse her. Nor did the sudden hole of dead silence in the ambient noise, as he touched his chest, though she tapped her earbud with a show of looking momentarily and mildly puzzled. "I could hardly say,

Master." She gave an obviously forced chuckle. "Nothing a relaxing vacation won't fix, I'm sure.

The top layer: I'm afraid I might have overstepped. The implication: Surely in your condition you're on the way to a rest cure?

"If you'll excuse me, sir." With a bow to him and the elders, she returned to the cockpit. She needed to see how much time she had. The obvious solution to her problem—to kill Milden—was impossible. She had neither strength nor training to defeat a Security man. She couldn't seal the Master cabin either. She'd angled to pilot this kind of carrier precisely because its open plan allowed sound to carry from the worker cabin into the cockpit.

As she took the pilot seat, the driver said, "Approaching the Bridge head, Master."

She opened the Master cabin mic. "Dear Master passengers, please allow the cabin servant to assist you in securing your safety harness." She began to order the worker cabin, "Put on your safety —"

Her external monitor flashed. Just in time, she stifled a Petro curse. She closed the mic. "Did you see that?" she whispered to the driver.

He gave a shaky laugh. "It looked like a garbage scow, Master."

"Yes. But what under the Doms is it doing…? Be sure to log it. There will be an investigation." With that bland assurance, she cleared her throat, opened the mic again and ordered the workers to harness in.

The scow had passed unnervingly close. Not nearly enough to collide. But a vessel passing close enough to be seen by another vessel—it just didn't happen.

Except it had happened.

Today.

She'd hardly taken it in when the floor began to vibrate so intensely, her feet tickled through her thick-soled safety shoes.

Movement on the monitors caught her attention again. Milden disappeared from the Master cabin monitor, reappeared in the worker cabin monitor. She hit auto and stood.

"Master," the driver said to her, "please don't leave your controls right now." His voice quivered. "I'm not authorized to adjust—"

"Hold steady, driver!"

In the monitor: Milden held something out. A weapon.

She rushed through to the worker cabin, but before she reached Milden, her foot caught a rolling cup. She lurched into the bar and tumbled to the floor.

A cacophony of sounds burst through the haze of pain. The child wailed. A tray of dishes smashed onto the floor. The elder-woman in the Master cabin cried, "What's happening?" over and over, while her husband repeated, his own voice shaking, "They're taking care of it."

Gasping, clinging to the bar, the Exile pulled herself to her feet. Reed's and Tyny's mouths moved, but the song faded as Milden's device analyzed and canceled it. Blu lay on his back, unconscious or dead, his mouth laced with foam, an orange dot on his neck.

Reed, despite the orange dot on his own coverall, poison sinking into his gut, punched Milden in the chest, then collapsed, dragging the Security Master down with him.

Exile staggered to them and rolled the young man away. Milden's eyes went blank, his mouth gaping, as smoke rose from the machine over his heart. Some lingering composure made her glad that the mother had covered the little girl's eyes. Milden spasmed so hard and fast, his head and heels made a tattoo worthy of a Security squad drill. Then he went limp.

Through it all, the weird notes cascaded flawlessly from Tyny's throat. She finished the tune, began it over.

But it wasn't working.

They should have been in stasis, "falling" through space: lost, off-Dom, silent. Dying.

They weren't. The carrier shuddered, paused, shuddered, paused. In a rhythm. The rhythm of the child's cries.

As the little girl gulped in air, the ship calmed. As she exhaled with a piercing wail, the ship trembled again. The shrill screams tweaked the song—canceling it or enhancing it, the Exile couldn't begin to guess. So bizarre, so unlikely, was this flaw in the plan, she would have been simply blank with astonishment, had she not been so desperate to fix it.

She grabbed the child easily—it was the last thing the mother expected. With one arm wrapped around the kicking girl's waist, the other hand stifling the wailing mouth, she struggled back to the Master cabin.

The girl's drawn up feet drummed on her abdomen. Her belly felt as if it would explode with pain each time one of the little heels connected, and the child's back arched with a force she would have thought beyond the strength of a toddler. Saliva, tears and mucus slicked the small face. It took every bit of the Exile's fortitude to keep hold of her. But the motions of the ship subsided.

Still clutching the child, the Exile flung herself into a seat. Thankfully, the servant planted himself at the Master cabin entry, doing his duty: keeping workers out.

Tyny sang on, bravely, perfectly.

The Exile panted to the elderly Master, "Turn my vid to outside."

He complied right away, age-spotted hand shaking. Fear and obedience to the shredding status quo quelled whatever questions he or his wife had about a Flight Master hauling a sobbing Worker child into their cabin.

The vid showed normal space.

All was well—from a Master's point of view. The conspiracy had failed.

The driver shouted, "We're going into stasis!"

She looked away from the screen as he turned to stare right into her eyes. Until this moment, she realized, she'd never truly believed it could happen.

"Prepare for landing!" the driver yelled, not bothering with the mics. "Everyone harness in! Secure loose objects!"

The child's struggles had weakened. The Flight Master looked down.

The blue tint of the little girl's face quenched her joy, as surely as Milden's device had canceled sound. She was killing this girl-child. But if she let her go…. Decades of conspiracy, transformation, training, of dangerous manipulations and plotting, the sacrifices of countless others, her husband's sacrifice—all could end in failure.

The little ruffle-trimmed legs and arms writhed, went limp, writhed again.

She lifted her hand.

The child gasped and choked and gasped—and let out a thin, piercing scream.

The external vid went white.

The Exile's mind went as white as the screen. Pulled back from the brink of triumph, she could not absorb the magnitude of failure.

The white gave way not to the metallic cleanliness of a Dominion port, nor to oblivion, but to a sparkling whirlwind. She drew in her breath, coughed as a gout of blood clogged her throat, swallowed hard, and cuddled the quieting girl.

A bright storm of sunlit sand and dust. A glimpse of refinery towers. The carrier touched down with a jolting bounce that would have thrown her and the little girl to the floor, had someone not harnessed them.

As if in a dream, she heard the driver talking into the radio, clicking one control after another.

"Dominion, do you read?" Click.

"Mayday." Click.

"Mayday." Click.

"Mayday." Click.

The whirlwind on the vid settled. The driver ran a full frequency test and got no response. He shut off power.

The craft was utterly silent, except for gasping breath from the passengers. The driver turned to face Exile. His face glowed ecstatic, terrified.

"Today is the day," he said.

She swallowed the blood in her throat. "Today is the day," she whispered back.

"Petro-09 is off-Dom." He said it more to himself than anyone else. "We're off-Dom. We're in a new country. We're free. We're free. We're free."

Touching down on an earth had not been part of the plan she knew. Her mind began to race, wondering if all the other earths.... But severed from the Dominions, she would never know if only this one earth had fallen free, or if earth after earth fell free with them. She knew only that she, three singers and the driver, and her husband, and countless other conspirators, whoever they were and however far-flung, had changed life forever, for everyone on Petro-09. Including herself.

She'd shed her gender, her features, her voice, movements, and mannerisms. She'd shed everything Petro of her. She'd peeled herself down to the core. She'd lived as an exile, trapped in a body hardly her own.

Now, she had to shed that, too. She was no longer an exile.

She cradled and kissed the sobbing child. "Sh-sh," she whispered. "It's all right now." She had barely the strength to hold the girl. The tiny, perfect feet in the shoes polished so lovingly by her mother or father had battered her mutilated organs.

The carrier flooded with light as the hatchway opened. The little girl's parents hovered at the Master cabin entry.

"Come in," she said. They did, timidly, and the father took his child.

"Walk me out," she ordered the mother. She corrected herself. "Would you please help me walk outside?" The mother hesitated, then put an arm around her waist and helped her to her feet. Together they walked down the ramp.

The carrier had landed near the refinery. But rather than a sallow haze of sour-acrid effluence, the sweet-spicy fragrance of pinyon filled a soaring sky of deep, bright, turquoise blue.

A strong wind had blown through Petro-09 this day.

Exile touched the earth and lifted her face to the warmth of the sun.

04 SECURITY MASTER'S STORY (SILENCE LIKE A THUNDERCLAP)

SECURITY MASTER DISMISSED the servant, waited until her scent dissipated, and cut a bite of his steak. Even washed up, made presentable for serving at tables, that body odor of workers clung to her, polluting the whiskey's bouquet.

He chewed the meat, sipped the whiskey. The good, amber spirit went perfectly with the steak.

Sweat. Dirt.

Not to mention the dining room's subtle reek of refinery fumes seeping through filtration. But that couldn't be helped.

"Mind if I join you?" Not awaiting an answer, S8 slung himself into the chair across the table. His eyes shone. Amped, Security Master guessed.

"Only if you chew with your mouth closed."

They ate, they chatted, they drank whiskey.

"Anything ever come of that killing in town?" S8 asked as the servant brought after-dinner cocktails.

"Religious rite of a chartered sect," Security answered.

"So we can't touch them."

"We can't touch them."

How the Faithful ever got a religious charter was beyond him. Officially, they expressed sub-Dominion convictions, but their true nature was that of a noxious, opportune weed. Typical of what thrived in the ugly, sun-blasted Petro sectors.

"Sometimes I wish I belonged to a cult like that," S8 said. "The pater won't let up about me flunking out of Academy."

They both laughed, though Security found no humor in S8's joke, with its implication that he would like to kill his father.

The servant brought another round.

As if that would bring freedom.

"I was at their church," Security said, "maybe minutes before it happened." He couldn't say why he mentioned it. S8 was the best friend Petro-09 had to offer, but Security never truly trusted him. Or even liked him.

"No shit." S8 enjoyed tossing out worker language.

"I went to audit the books."

"Right." S8 gave a snort.

Given that the church's revenues ranged from minuscule to in-significant, everyone, including the Faithful themselves, knew that audits were really surveillance calls.

"I plied my trade in the so-called office. A cafeteria table for a desk. Chairs discarded from a smoking lobby. A joke of an office."

He blathered about office furniture, but it was the preacher's face that held his mind's eye. Calm and tired. Weathered. Steadfast.

"How were the books?" S8 asked.

Faithful.

"Perfect."

S8 gulped his drink. "They keep their books perfect, then turn around and murder each other."

"I almost ran into the son on the way out of the place."

Not that they would literally have run into each other. He hadn't realized the son was waiting right outside, but the son had certainly known of a Master's presence. He'd stood well back as Security came out of the "office."

"Did he look vicious?" S8 stuck a finger in his glass, whirled the ice around.

"No. He looked like they all do."

"Like any Petro, in other words."

Like all the Faithful do, Security had meant. Not like any Petro. He'd looked different, even, from the rest of the Faithful. They would look different, wouldn't they, preacher and son, with one likely to kill the other any time. But that wasn't how they looked, either.

"I can't tell them apart." S8 brayed a laugh. "Even the boys from the girls, sometimes."

The son had glanced him up and down in that way they had—looking but not seeming to look—with contempt untainted by harshness or malice.

"I would recognize him if I saw him again." Why was he going on about this? "But I doubt he would recognize me."

"I bet he would." S8 shook an ice chunk into his mouth. "They don't see many of us around."

"Too hot out there for the likes of us," Security said. "No air conditioning."

"No ice for our drinks," S8 said.

The servant, approaching with another round, hesitated, confused. "You don't want ice in—?"

"Ice is fine," Security said.

S8 stared her back to the bar, a buxom girl in tight, revealing clothes, then returned to Security. "I wonder what happens if the father does the killing? Or if he doesn't have a son at all. What happens when he dies?"

"They import a preacher from another sector. That's how this pair ended up here. Shipped over from Petro-10."

The father had killed his own father, on P-10. He was a murderer. He also happened to be a senior hostler, skilled, dependable, hard-working, and with an excellent safety record. When the Faithful on P-09 requested a preacher, he got bumped up a degree.

S8 raised his glass. "To Religious Diversity."

"Religious Diversity." He lifted his glass—

Everything went silent.

They froze, glasses still raised. Security could hear his own ears ringing, his blood pulsing. A soft clink as melting ice slipped in the drink.

Security dropped his glass and strode to the entry, checking his weapon, forgetting S8, forgetting the servant and the drinks and the tender steak done just right. He ran along the passage, dodging people straggling from dwellings or rec rooms. A small phalanx of subordinate Security Masters joined him.

"Audio's dead," one of them said as they jogged toward the facility.

"Where's Leader Falc?" he demanded.

"Out there," another said.

"Out there" meant in the plant. That was bad. Or maybe not. Without Falc, things would go more smoothly. Whatever "things" were. No alarms sounded, no emergency lights flashed. The dead audio, the unmoving air, the dimness of the corridor made the most frantic alarm.

No ice for drinks.

He raised a hand to signal a halt as they reached the hatch to the facility. The monitors dark, he reached for the Master control. He flicked through the channels. Dark. Dark. Dark. Dark. All dark. Clearly, this was no ordinary malfunction.

This was something like chaos.

"Someone in the plant covered the vids," one of the detail said wonderingly. "Every last one of them."

How could they have found them all? Concealed in ducts, ventilation screens, lighting fixtures, roof struts…. Never mind. That was a mystery to solve later.

The environmental sensors functioned, at least. Atmosphere in the plant: temperatures up slightly. Heavy volume in shipping and receiving could warm up the facility, the bays open all day. But today's freight schedule had been light.

Without surveillance, no telling what was going on in there. Out there, rather. Security tried calling Central Comm on the manual wall-phone. He neither hoped for nor received an answer.

As a cadet, he'd trained for uprisings, rebellions, slow-downs, accidents, industrial and natural disasters. Whether this was a rebellion or an industrial disaster wasn't yet clear. What did manifest with perfect clarity was the inadequacy, the downright idiocy of the training. The drills implemented communications systems, cleverly hidden monitors, remote-controlled hatches, shut-down combinations, sprinkler systems delivering chemicals deadly or merely sedating. Things that did what was needed with touches on clearly lit panels.

None of these would work for the Masters, this day. Nothing would work for the Masters from this day forward. He knew it. The silence told him. Screamed it at him.

Panic seeped over the faces of the Security detail, much as they tried to hide it. They kept touching their earbuds, a sort of group twitch. One went so far as to remove his, shake it, scrape the mic with his fingernail. They'd never heard silence, ever in their lives.

Security had. Once, on border patrol, he'd removed his earbuds. Not exactly silence. A soft, swelling and falling whistling. Rustles of what he's assumed was something creeping through the dried grass. He'd never done it again, and he'd never spoken of it.

He issued brisk instructions. Go check Central Comm. Go to the main control room. Go inform this or that person. Go here. Go there. He fragmented them without telling why: they had no chance of surviving as a group. Each would have to fend for himself. He didn't expect many, if any at all, to make it. Most would probably disobey orders. They'd flock to safe rooms no longer safe, trotting along the corridors like livestock to a feedlot.

Alone, he went to his quarters. He ripped open his pillow and rooted out the pass stone hidden there. Strange, the feeling of not being watched. He started to shove the stone in his pocket, but placed it on the nightstand instead. How it sparkled.

He stripped off his uniform and removed the patches and badges, then put the uniform back on. He would have changed into civilian clothes, but the uniform had big pockets, and its rugged fabric would better withstand Petro conditions. It didn't matter anyway, what he wore, tearing off the patches and badges. He could be buck naked, and any worker would peg him as Security. It was as if, in cadet school, he'd been re-featured to his role. He considered and discarded the idea of wearing armor. He donned a broad-brimmed hat.

Could this be happening? Or was he crazy?

He filled his pockets with snacks. When he searched his mind for what else to carry, he discovered an encroaching panic that threatened to rout any logical train of thought. He sat again, breathed in, breathed out. In. Out.…

Water. He would need water. How to carry it? Potable liquids got shipped in kegs. In the Masters' area, it flowed from taps into glasses and cups. Only warehouse workers used canteens, a productivity enhancement to keep them from loitering at water kegs. He mindlessly upended drawers, boxes, rooted through his closet. Nothing.

He stood defeated, a few feathers wafting around him, the stone clenched in his hand.

He hadn't trusted it to the safe. Nights, feigning sleep, he'd worked the pillow's stitches loose, making a slit big enough for his hand, and worked it into a feathered nest.

The Mixed he'd taken it from had blurted, It's a moon rock! Then, more sensibly, and correctly, he said it wasn't his, said it was a gemstone, stolen from Dom knew where and planted on him by Dom knew whom. Security had recognized it for what it was. No more a gemstone than a moon rock, it was a pass stone that opened all doors.

Security had killed the Mixed, taken the stone. No one raised questions over the border death of a Mixed. No one even claimed the body.

All that was fine. No problem. Except he hadn't gotten to the stupid part yet. Which was, for all his precautions, he hadn't figured out what really happened, with that Mixed at the border. Never understood. Blinded by his own greed, or whatever it was, it never dawned on him: he'd caught the Mixed on the way *out* of the plant, not on the way in.

The blacked-out vids. The dead audio-comms. The stuck passways.

The desperate bustle over, silence rose again. He yanked out his dead earbuds.

Of the one hundred Masters stationed on Petro-09, about a third would be in the plant. Another third would be asleep, or sitting bolt upright in their beds, wondering what woke them, not realizing that silence could be like a thunderclap. If they even knew what a thunderclap was. A handful would be on border patrol or at leisure, as he and S8 had been. The rest were heading for safe rooms, or already making themselves at home in them. What it would be like in those rooms—in the whole facility—when the lack of climate control became apparent, he didn't like to imagine.

And he wasn't staying to find out. The plan: get out of here. Escape. If anything that once worked still worked.

He shoved the stone in his trousers pocket.

He reached the wing's external exit without meeting anyone else, worker or Master. The pass stone sprang the door open. Security looked outside without releasing the door.

The blank perimeter of the facility stretched into a seemingly endless distance.

Security stepped out, and the door snapped shut. He began to turn back, to see if the pass stone would open it from this side, then stopped himself. The pass stone would work from this side, he decided. He didn't test this decision.

The sun hung low by the time the Shipping pad came in sight. His mouth was parched. His legs shook. He'd never slacked on the exercise regime mandated for Security, but he'd never walked this far, either. Not in his whole life. He'd had a vehicle, for border patrol.

A group of workers approached. They seemed to have sprung out of the dirt, out of nowhere. He didn't try to run. Eventually, they surrounded him.

"I have a gemstone. A pass stone, I mean." It was babble, he knew, even as he pointed back the way he'd come. "It'll get you in. Back there. The residential wing."

A man he recognized as the Faithful son nodded and told him, in the friendliest manner imaginable, what he already knew. "We're off-Dom."

"We're free," added a driver. A passenger-carrier driver, Security noted, and not the only odd member of the group. A little kid and her parents: domestics. A woman pilot carried on a chair—a Master, to boot. Workers from the plant. Two ancient looking Masters. He searched their faces for deference, for need, for mercy. For something they might hold in common. He surely smelled like them. Sweat and dirt.

But the reek of fear—that was entirely his.

05 SALOON KEEPER'S STORY (TRADE)

A BREEZE STIRRED at the top of the bluff, but the sun made Roudo sweat. Maybe nerves, a little. The amps kicking in. He kept his hands in sight. No peace ties on the weapons, in this forum, and Ray was a quick draw. Quicker than his daddy, for sure. Ray'd shot him through the chest right smartly, then stepped up to the pulpit. Faithful. Not a man to tangle with. Roudo's guards stood at ready, but that wouldn't save him from Ray's first shot.

The quietness got on Roudo's nerves more than the way Ray's hands rested on his weapon handles. This far from town, even the turbines' squawking couldn't be heard. The refinery shut down, too. Unreal. The sound that rocked his cradle, gone. Three weeks, now, and still it felt like half the world had been lopped off. He'd never noticed before how amps roar through your ears.

The question didn't need to be asked: what do you want? Roudo already knew that.

"Where you all headed?" Roudo asked, though he knew the answer to this, too.

"New country."

"Today's the day, huh."

Ray looked surprised that he knew about that.

"Mmhm," Roudo said, as if omniscient.

Actually, at the saloon one night, a lapsed Faithful had retailed the twaddle of New Country, to much merriment. When the day comes, the Faithful would migrate off-sector to some mysterious land. There they would figure out a way to process plants and animals for food. That part of it sounded more like an Ag sector than any kind of paradise. They'd have to clothe and shelter themselves. No supplies, and nary a pill to get them through their toils. Then at the end of each wearisome day, they'd fall asleep any old where, with no respect to age, gender, or shift. No doubt about it, religious people cherished the most idiotic, far-flung crap.

Gross crap, actually. Roudo had pulled some nasty tricks in his time, but killing his father? Much as he'd hated the crusty old bastard, he'd at least allowed him to do the job himself, smoking, drinking, fighting, and amping himself to that final journey, the gurney ride to the retort.

Roudo had a way, he knew, of staring off somewhere unknown. It was just the amps whirling around in his head. Let people assume it to be a fit of deep thought. He came back to the situation with a show of deliberation, as if he'd been making a weighty decision.

Maybe he actually had made a weighty decision. His people— the Petros were now his people—wouldn't live like that.

"You going off sector, you'll need supplies," Roudo said. True, but that wasn't what Ray was after. Roudo had brought Pru along, with one of his men assigned to watch her, just in case.

Ray was the one to watch, though, and not just because he hadn't taken his hands from his weapons. Religion had evidently rotted parts of his brain, but he wasn't entirely witless. And he had quick hands. Roudo once spotted Ray palming a card, smooth as can be. Had Roudo been playing, not watching from the bar, he never would've caught it.

Ray reached out his hand. As if to prove Roudo's thoughts, it was empty, then suddenly not empty.

On Ray's palm lay a smooth, sparkling stone. Roudo could just about hear it catching the sunlight and throwing it back out in little sparks. The quietness allowed it. Or again, it could have been the amps. Despite the wonder of it all, Roudo didn't miss that the Security Master at Ray's elbow literally twitched at the sight of it.

"Sweet," Roudo said. "Almost as good as your palming cards."

Ray lifted his eyebrows. "Not so great, if you saw me."

"A saloon keeper's gotta have a sharp eye."

Ray flipped the gemstone through his fingers. "Yours." And with that, his dick took over negotiations. "For Pru."

Roudo kept his game face. "That's right handsome of you, Ray, but blessed if I know what to do with a pretty rock. Necessities being the latest currency."

Ray scanned Roudo's face, as if they were at the card table. "What's your price, then?" Dexterity had never overcome his utter lack of subtlety.

"Your Security man."

Who was eying Pru. Something about her. If you don't like the crooked nose and missing teeth, turn out the light.

Ray opened his mouth to answer when Pru stepped forward. "No," she said.

Judging from Ray's expression, nothing could have surprised him more.

And nothing could have irritated Roudo more. He didn't give her the back of his hand, however. Never let anyone say old Roudo didn't exert some willpower now and then.

"Shut up and step down, you silly bitch." It gave his manly parts a sweet little stir, that she'd come all this way to let Ray know she belonged to her old keeper. But no matter. If Ray wanted to swap his Security man for a whore, done and done.

Pitiful specimen that he was, this Security Master. Sweat dripped off his hair and circled his armpits. Roudo almost expected to see a brown stain on his britches. Maybe they were all like that, cut off from the Doms. But he was the only Master that Roudo had seen since Petro-09 went off-line. Dead or alive, the rest must be inside the Masters' wing of the plant.

That was where Roudo wanted to be. He'd heard about life inside the Masters' wing. Big soft beds, barrels of booze, a pharmacy, and who knew what goodies to eat. But Roudo had done everything he could to get in, from axes to tree trunks. He'd even blown up an oil drum at one of the hatches. The place was sealed tight. If anybody could get in, it would be Security. Then again, Ray just came from the plant. He would've tried that angle....

The stone. Roudo would've kicked himself, had he not been so busy not laughing at Ray, who might be smart enough, in his way, but hadn't figured out what he was playing with. The rock was a pass stone. A key to the plant. Sure, that's what it was. It didn't have a natural look, even for a honed mineral.

While Ray endowed Pru with a burning, lovelorn stare, Security took a long, hard look at Roudo, which Roudo met with a raised eyebrow.

"I'll stay here with your outfit," Security said to Roudo.

It wouldn't do to yell, "Hot shit!" or pump his fist in the air. The thing was to let Security know that old Roudo was the one who decided who stayed with his outfit.

Roudo gestured one of his men to hand his weapon to Security, then scanned the plain below the bluff. He spotted a half-dead tamarisk. "Shoot that nest out of yonder tree."

Security took the weapon, raised it, and shot, all in one smooth movement. The nest flew out of the tree, birdies and all. Best yet, Security made to hand the weapon back to Roudo.

"Keep it."

Roudo wasn't prompted by the warm feeling in his heart, though he did, literally, have a nice cozy feeling there. He wanted Security to take rank asap.

"You want the rock?" Security asked Roudo.

"Oh, yes."

Ray looked from Roudo to Security and back, then handed the rock over.

Roudo pocketed it. What did the Book call it? Serendipity. He had Security, and a pass stone, for nothing. No, he'd leave the pallet of supplies. It was the nice thing to do. And it wasn't worth killing themselves hauling back four kegs of expired fuel and a couple dozen cases of dated chow.

"Good luck to you, Ray."

Ray managed, "Back at you, Roudo," all fallen apart as he evidently was, the whore and Security having opted for sanity.

The sunny air soon filled with the sounds of labor as the Faithful began loading fuel packets onto their already over-burdened vehicles.

Roudo's group wended its way back up the bluff. He would have put Security at the rear, but he doubted Ray would do anything untoward. More prudent to put Security on point, where the bodyguards could keep an eye on him, til he proved himself trustworthy. Confiscating Security's weapon wouldn't send the right message. Security was slated to be his number one, and the sooner the position was established, the better.

Being in management was like playing high-stakes. Every move a gamble that you could win big or lose big.

Halfway up the bluff, Roudo paused to look back down. The Faithful were moving on, leaving the pallet half-loaded. Presumably they'd given up on it, or they planned to come back from their land of plenty to retrieve the rest.

"Faithful!" Pru's shout broke the quiet.

Shit if she wasn't making her way down the bluff.

Roudo hadn't bothered to keep an eye on her. After all, she'd said no to the trade. He'd logically assumed she wanted to stay his. Looked like she'd changed her mind. Ray headed toward Pru, walking fast.

A movement: Security cocking his weapon. Roudo's amped up heart gave a painful bound—Ray set him up!—then he breathed out. Security had sited on the touching scene. Every line of him honed to kill. Superb.

"Shall I shoot?" Security asked. Honed to kill on command.

Roudo considered the situation, the amps coursing a jagged joy through his body and mind. He'd first leaped to the conclusion that Security meant: shoot Pru. But only a fool would waste ammo on her. Security had raised his weapon after Ray separated from the flock of Faithful.

"How long before they're out of range, once they start moving again?" Roudo asked.

"You have a couple of minutes."

Roudo nodded, pleased with the answer, pleased with the way it was phrased.

If Security assassinated Ray, the Faithful would be like a headless snake, writhing for a while, then expiring. On the other hand....

"Nah." Roudo shook his head. "Let him go. An Ag sector will come in handy, a couple years from now."

"Him, I don't understand." Security faced Roudo. "You, I do understand. You know how things work."

Roudo's grin faded.

Someone laughed.

The bright morning ended.

06 THE NEW WOMAN'S STORY (TODAY'S THE DAY)

SHE WALKED TO her new people without looking back. Her legs shook so hard, the rocky ground seemed to lurch under her feet. The certainty of a weapon aimed at her back pressed between her shoulder blades like the fist of a man.

A hundred stories played out in her mind, of fists and rotten teeth and dirty beds.

Leave it behind, she told herself. Leave it forever, even if you die doing it.

Leave it!

She didn't want to die, didn't want the weapon pointed at her back to blast her apart, as it had the little nest. She wanted to live. When she'd joined the Faithful, leaving town, she'd vowed to herself, that she would live not only for the children she might have, but for all the Faithful. She would live to break the chain of death that enslaved them.

Even before the shot had a chance to echo, her palms and knees scraped hard over the rough dirt. She hadn't fallen, though. She'd dropped to the ground. She was alive. Crouching, she looked back up the bluff.

The Security Master… The man in the Security outfit waved down at her, gestured with his gun toward the ground at his feet. Roudo lay sprawled, one of his arms dangling limp over the edge of the bluff, streaks of blood darkened the dust there. The man waved again, then turned away. Some of the others with him glanced down. A woman put a foot to Roudo's body, as if to push it down, but the man said something, and she shrugged and left it. They all then followed him away, leaving Roudo to finish dying alone.

They would be going back to the refinery. The thought of what surely awaited them there made her shudder. It was the fate they chose, just as she'd chosen hers. She stood, her legs wobbly.

Ray took her hands, the sun strong on his face.

"I had to come to you free," she told him. "I had to keep the promise we made to each other, that night on the rock.

Shame darkened his eyes like a shadow running over the sun. He'd broken that promise, when he offered to trade an object for her. She made no accusation, though. There was no shame in what he'd done. Born a slave, lived a slave—it was all they'd known.

She'd gathered every scrap of her courage, to refuse to be an article of barter, to take the only freedom ever offered her, even as she'd condemned herself, so she thought, to lifelong degradation and bondage. Then she'd realized something truly wonderful. She had more courage to spare!

He'd broken their promise, but she'd mended it.

SARAG ENDS THE STORY

AND THEY ALL lived happily ever after.

Right? Isn't that what you children want?

Then stop jabbering and bring me a hookah and a cactus brew — with the lime fresh-squeezed. Give an old lady her reward.

••• •••

About Jean Huets

JEAN HUETS' WRITING has been published in *The New York Times, The Brooklyn Rail, The Millions, Ploughshares, Kenyon Review, North American Review, Civil War Monitor*, and other journals. She is author of *With Walt Whitman, Himself*, acclaimed as "a book of marvels" by poet Steve Scafidi; *The Cosmic Tarot* book, based on the visionary art of Norbert Loesche, *Alt Sagas: Stories*, and *The Bones You Have Cast Down: A Novel*; and co-author, with Stuart R. Kaplan, of *The Encyclopedia of Tarot*. She co-founded Circling Rivers press.

www.ingramcontent.com/pod-product-compliance
Lightning Source LLC
Chambersburg PA
CBHW061439210726

48287CB00007B/2277